"But why ad

"You're an attra
plenty of wom
pleased to—" Nicole quickly stopped
herself from saying *step into your wife's
shoes.* It was too insensitive. Ross was still
hurting deeply.

"I have no wish to go through the
preliminaries of dating and wooing."

"So what is it that you want?"

"My main aim is to make my aunt Matilda
happy. She's terminally ill and her dearest
ambition is to see me married again."

Nicole's eyes widened. "And you'd do
that? You'd marry a complete stranger
to make your aunt happy?" It was a very
noble gesture; it could also be the biggest
mistake of his life.

Born in the industrial heart of England, **MARGARET MAYO** now lives in a Staffordshire countryside village. She became a writer by accident after attempting to write a short story when she was almost forty, and now writing is one of the most enjoyable parts of her life. She combines her hobby of photography with her research.

Margaret Mayo

MARRIAGE BY CONTRACT

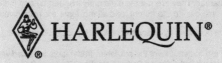

HARLEQUIN®

TORONTO • NEW YORK • LONDON
AMSTERDAM • PARIS • SYDNEY • HAMBURG
STOCKHOLM • ATHENS • TOKYO • MILAN • MADRID
PRAGUE • WARSAW • BUDAPEST • AUCKLAND

ISBN 0-373-18767-X

MARRIAGE BY CONTRACT

First North American Publication 2001.

Visit us at www.eHarlequin.com

Printed in U.S.A.

CHAPTER ONE

'HEY, girls, listen to this.' Terri looked up from the newspaper. 'There's a guy here advertising for a wife.'

'You're joking!' Marie paused from painting her toenails. 'Why would anyone want to marry a complete stranger? He'll never get any takers—unless they're desperate, of course.

'Perhaps *he* is desperate?' Nicole, the third member of the group, cradled her coffee mug in her hands and looked at her flatmates thoughtfully. 'Perhaps he has a very good reason for wanting a wife.'

'Trust you to think something like that.'

Nicole shrugged. 'Things aren't always what they seem. It's a drastic measure. He must have a huge problem.'

'Yeah, like maybe he's in line for an inheritance,' scoffed Marie.

'Or he's as ugly as sin and as old as Methuselah but wants to produce an heir.' Terri shuddered. 'Fancy going to bed with someone like that. I wouldn't do it for a million pounds, not even ten million.'

'Is he offering money?' asked Marie.

'I don't know. I don't think so.' Terri studied the newspaper again.

'Well, I think you shouldn't make fun of him when you don't know the true facts,' Nicole said with quiet determination.

'Listen to you,' derided Marie.

'Why don't you answer the ad and find out?' suggested Terri slyly.

'I might just do that,' said Nicole with a faint smile.

5

Her friends looked at her with their mouths dropping open. 'You cannot be serious?'

'Of course I'm not.' She laughed now. 'But I'd really love to find out why he feels it necessary to advertise for a wife.

'It's her journalistic instinct,' stated Marie.

'No, it's not.'

'Then what is it?'

Nicole shrugged. 'Just interest.'

'Do a story on it, then,' urged Terri. 'Go and see him; find out what makes the man tick.'

'I might just do that.' Nicole nodded her head slowly and consideringly.

Having walked out on her job at the local newspaper, she planned to freelance until she found something else— preferably with an editor who didn't think she had no brain, who didn't think she was there for his pleasure. A shudder ran through her at the thought of Simon Snell's groping hands.

'Pass me the paper,' she said to Terri. 'I want to see if there's a number.'

Terri scanned the advertisement for the third time. 'Yes, there is. Over to you.'

Nicole read it intently before finally dialling.

'Dufrais. Sorry I'm out. Leave your name and number and I'll—'

An answer-machine! She hated them and had no intention of speaking to a machine. But the message was suddenly interrupted. 'Dufrais here. Who's calling?'

The voice was gruff and impatient and it did nothing to convince Nicole to carry on with the call. If he was the one advertising for a wife then he wasn't doing a very good job of convincing his respondents that he was good husband material.

But nothing ventured, nothing gained. She took a deep

breath. 'My name is Nicole Quest. I'm ringing about your advertisement.'

'Oh!'

'What do you mean, "oh"?' she asked. 'Have I got the right number or haven't I?' She looked at her friends and pulled a mystified face.

'Yes, you have the right number, but the ad should never have been put in.'

'In that case I'm wasting my time.' She was about to slam down the phone when he spoke again.

'When can you come and see me?' His voice was quiet and resigned now, as though he felt obliged, but it didn't soothe Nicole's ruffled feathers.

'And I always thought it was the female sex who had the prerogative to change their minds,' she said cuttingly. He didn't respond so she went on, 'I can come just as soon as you like Mr—er—Dufrais.'

She was intrigued now, wanted to see what this guy looked like, find out what sort of a person had penned such an advertisement and then had second thoughts. Why did he need a wife? And why had he gone about it in such a strange way?

'Good, I'll expect you in—what? Half an hour?'

'It depends where you live.'

'Of course.'

He gave her his address and Nicole scribbled it down, saying as she did so, 'That's not too far. I can be there in twenty minutes.'

The cottage was in a delightful spot overlooking the estuary at St Meek, near Bude, the end one in a row of what had once been fishermen's cottages. High tide had turned the estuary into a vast lake, where a couple of derelict boats bobbed forlornly and seagulls wheeled and squealed, but other than that there was no sign of life.

Nicole stopped her car and studied the cottage. It was

bigger than its neighbours, probably two knocked into one.
The garden was overgrown, the woodwork in need of painting, and the stone walls that had once been painted white
were now a dirty grey. The mullioned windows, however,
were well polished; twinkling and sparkling in the evening
sunshine.

All of a sudden the faded blue door swung open and a
man in a red sweater and dark trousers stepped out. 'Nicole
Quest, I presume? Are you going to sit there all day?' He
sounded as impossible as he had on the phone.

Nicole opened the door and swung her legs out, taking
her time, assessing him as she did so. Tall, in his mid to
late thirties, dark dishevelled hair, a sculpted face that
looked as though the artist had forgotten to round off the
angles. A little too thin, and extremely sad-looking.

Something had happened to this man. Something very
tragic. It was there in the lifeless eyes, in the weariness that
encompassed him. Her journalistic mind worked overtime.
She could smell a story already.

She held out her hand as she approached him. 'Mr
Dufrais?'

'That's right, but call me Ross,' he suggested roughly,
ignoring her hand. 'You'd best come in.' His dark eyes
observed her swiftly, not missing one inch of her slender
body, or the short dark hair that framed her heart-shaped
face and gave her an elfin look.

He took her through to a room where floor-length windows opened on to a stone terrace with fantastic views of
the estuary. The carpet was ocean-green, the walls cream,
and the sofa and easy chairs were in a boldly patterned
fabric in purple, cream and the same shade of green. A
woman's touch here, she thought. But who?

It was a long, narrow room—obviously two of the orig-
inal rooms knocked into one—with a walnut dresser and a
hi-fi unit against one wall and a console table against an-

other. The day's newspapers were lying around—as were a few children's toys.

A child! Was it his? Was he a divorcee? Did he want to marry again for the sake of his child? They were questions she was dying to ask.

'Sit down,' he said, still looking at her intently. 'Tell me about yourself.'

Nicole perched on the edge of the nearest chair, ankles neatly crossed, handbag on the floor beside her, keeping her wide-spaced blue eyes directly on his. 'Actually, I'd like to hear about you first. I think it only fair that I should know why you're advertising for a wife. It's very unusual to say the least.'

He had taken the chair opposite but he wasn't relaxed. He sat forward, his head bowed, appearing to consider her question, his hands linked loosely between his parted knees. He was so long in answering that Nicole wondered whether she ought to remind him that she was waiting.

Finally he said, 'My wife and daughter died twelve months ago. I have to get on with my life.' He spoke like a robot, as though he'd conditioned himself to finding someone to take his wife's place. As though it was something he felt he ought to do, but in fact was the last thing he wanted.

'But why *advertise* for someone? You're an attractive man; you must know plenty of women who'd be only too pleased to—' She quickly stopped herself from saying, Step into your wife's shoes. It was too insensitive. He was still hurting deeply.

'I have no wish to go through the preliminaries of dating and wooing.'

'So what is it that you want?' Sharpness edged her voice.

'My main aim is to make Matilda happy.'

'Matilda?' Who was she? What had she got to do with his getting married?

'She's my aunt.'

'Oh, I see.' In fact she didn't see anything at all. 'Why is her happiness so important to you?'

'She has a terminal illness.'

Oh, hell, tragedy heaped on tragedy. No wonder he looked tired and defeated. But did she want to be involved in any of this?

'And her dearest ambition is to see me married again.'

Nicole's eyes widened. 'And you'd do that? You'd marry a complete stranger to make your aunt happy?' It was a very noble gesture; it could also be a very stupid one. It could be the biggest mistake of his life.

'I also need someone to look after Aaron.'

Ah! The child! His surviving son! She'd love to know how his wife and daughter had died. It was a terrible thing. But what he was doing wasn't much better. He couldn't just force a new mother on the child; it wouldn't work.

'Tilda's no longer capable, and I cannot be here all of the time.'

'So you thought you'd kill two birds with one stone, so to speak?' She arched her finely shaped brows, her wide-spaced blue eyes cool and questioning.

'I guess that's about it.'

'I suppose you want someone to fulfil your physical needs as well, but with none of the complications of love?' she asked scathingly. This man had to be living in cloud-cuckoo-land if he thought any woman would meet those demands. Women liked commitment and love. Women were emotional creatures. They couldn't turn their feelings on and off at will.

His answer surprised her. 'No, that's not what I'm saying at all.' There was impatience in his tone, his dark eyes flicking disdainfully over her. 'It will be purely a business deal. I shan't expect my chosen wife to go to bed with me.'

'But you'll expect her to give up her liberties?' she countered, indigo-blue eyes deeply judgemental.

He closed heavy lids for a moment, as though finding her questions extremely tiresome. 'Well, yes, it will be a full-time job. But I shall pay well in return.'

'What do you have against love, Mr Dufrais?'

It was a question he hadn't expected and obviously didn't like. He dragged his dark brows together and thrust disparagingly, 'Love, Miss Quest? Love is a destructive emotion. It has no part to play in my life.'

She was a little taken aback by his vehemence. 'Didn't you love your wife?'

He looked ready to explode. 'What sort of a damn fool question is that? Of course I loved her.'

'And yet you're proposing to take another wife without letting emotions enter into it.' She didn't understand this man at all.

'It is best.' His deep-set black eyes warned her that she was treading on dangerous ground and that no further questions were acceptable.

This was going to make a superb human-interest story, thought Nicole. A loveless marriage for the sake of his aunt and child.

It was a selfless action in one respect, but also extremely selfish in another, to expect some woman to put her life on hold for an indeterminate length of time. It was something she couldn't imagine herself doing. Nor, she felt sure, would many others.

'Do you like children?'

Nicole had been so busy committing everything he said to memory, wishing she had thought to bring her tape recorder, that she almost missed the question. 'Do I like children?' she repeated. 'You didn't put that in your ad.'

'Meaning you don't. OK.' He jumped to his feet. 'You may go.'

Astonished by his sudden and unexpected reaction, Nicole said firmly, 'I didn't say that.'

'But you implied it.' He looked down at her, black eyes impaling, condemning, his whole body taut.

'I merely mentioned that you didn't ask it.' She kept her tone calm and friendly. 'I actually happen to like children, though some of your applicants may not. You may have misled them.'

'Hmph!' he snorted, but she could see that he accepted her point. He sat down again, and this time he stretched out his long legs in front of him, leaning back in the chair and folding his arms across his wide chest. 'Do you have a boyfriend?'

Nicole shook her head. 'No.' She studied his shadowed face. Pale and gaunt, heavy rings under his eyes as though he needed to sleep for a week. Obviously looking after a sick aunt and a young son was taking its toll. He needed a nurse and a nanny, not a wife.

'How long since you finished your last relationship?' he asked tersely. 'I want no irate ex-lovers breathing down my neck.'

'There's been no one for a long time,' she answered with a faint wry smile, inwardly deciding how she was going to write his story. She needed a lot more details; it would take careful questioning and he mustn't guess what she was up to. But already ideas were beginning to formulate...

'So you've no ties, nothing to stop you uprooting and coming to live with me?'

'None.' And pigs would fly. Did he really think any girl would tie herself to him just like that? Unless he was offering some phenomenal wage.

'How about your job?'

'I don't have one,' she told him.

Brows rose. 'You're unemployed? You're wondering

how much you can get out of this. Is that it?' There was sudden sharp accusation in his tone.

Nicole shook her head, eyes sparking fiercely. 'No, that is not it. I walked out on my job today, as a matter of fact. I was being sexually harassed. And I never thought of money when I rang about your advert.'

Ross looked at her through narrowed eyes for several long seconds, seeming as though he wanted to ask exactly why she had responded, but instead he said, 'Are you suing? Will there be an ongoing problem?'

'No.' She couldn't help thinking what beautiful eyes he had—if they weren't so sad! Dark, dark brown, almost black, and the whites were clear, his lashes long and thick. 'I don't intend taking it any further. He's not worth it.'

He nodded, accepting her word, asking no more questions, much to her relief. He was presumably so tied up in his own problems that what had happened to her was of no importance. 'So, a little about yourself,' he went on. 'I need a wife who can entertain when necessary, someone who can hold a decent conversation, someone intelligent.'

Nicole's blue eyes flashed yet again. 'I left school with straight As. And I got first-class honours at university,' she retorted icily. 'Is that sufficient?' He gave the briefest of nods, not particularly impressed, but satisfied with what she'd told him. 'How are you at acting?' He was still far from relaxed, his fingers interlinked, thumbs constantly moving. Uncomfortable with the interview. Probably wishing he'd never started this whole thing.

'Acting?' She knew she sounded dumb but it was such an unexpected question.

'Yes, acting.' He gave a sigh of impatience. 'You'll need to pretend to be in love with me when the occasion demands it. Could you do that?' He stood as he spoke and moved closer, looking down at her with hard lines of concentration on his face.

It was Nicole's turn to feel uncomfortable. Was he seriously considering her for the job? She hadn't thought that far. She'd been more interested in why he'd placed the ad, in the story she'd get out of it.

'I think the question is, could *you* do it?' she asked instead of answering. 'You're the one who has to convince everyone that you're happily married again, especially Aaron. Kids pick up on these things, you know. Have you thought of it from his point of view?'

Judging by his quick frown he hadn't, and Nicole got the impression that he hadn't thought this thing through at all.

'Aaron's too young to understand,' he defended.

'I don't think so,' she said. 'How old is he?'

'Three, almost four.'

'So he was two when—?'

'When his mother died? Yes.'

'Does he remember her?'

'I make sure that he does. I think it's important.'

'So how will it affect him when he suddenly gets a new—'

The door burst open and a small boy hurtled into the room and threw himself at Ross.

A smile transformed Ross's face; his arms opened wide. He'd said love had no part to play in his life, but he certainly had heaps for this child.

'Grandpa, Grandpa, look.' Aaron held up a bandaged finger. 'I cut it but I didn't cry.'

Grandpa! To say Nicole was shocked was putting it mildly. This she certainly hadn't expected.

'You're very brave.' Ross duly inspected the heavily bandaged finger. 'But I did say that you weren't to interrupt me.'

'But, Grandpa—' Tears began to well.

'Unless it was very important,' added Ross. 'And I guess this is.'

Aaron nodded solemnly and then looked directly at Nicole. There was no hint of shyness on his scrubbed and shining face. His dark hair was neatly brushed and he had Ross's beautiful eyes. 'Are you Grandpa's new girlfriend?'

Nicole was still trying to come to terms with the fact that Aaron wasn't Ross's son, and when this question was delivered she was for once at a loss for words.

'*Aaron!*' A look of horror crossed Ross's face. 'That's very rude.'

'But Tilda said that—'

'It doesn't matter what Tilda said.'

'But, Grandpa—'

'Aaron, that's enough.'

The little boy's face crumpled and Nicole felt sorry for him. 'I think I have some sweets in my bag,' she said quickly. 'Would you like one?'

He looked at his grandfather for permission, and when given he slipped off his lap and ran eagerly over to Nicole. She searched for the tube of wine gums and gave them to him. He took one and handed it back.

'You can keep them if you like.'

'All of them?' His dark eyes looked at her hopefully.

'Yes.'

'Ooh, thank you.' He ran back to his grandfather. 'Look what I've got.'

'What a lucky young man you are. Why don't you go and show Tilda?'

'Tilda's asleep.'

Ross frowned. 'Go and play in your room, then; there's a good boy. I'll be with you shortly.'

'Can I show the lady my new cars?'

'No.'

Aaron's bottom lip began to quiver.

'Perhaps another time,' said Nicole, feeling sorry for the youngster.

Ross glared, and she knew he thought she was being presumptuous. But she wasn't; she knew there wouldn't be another time. She was only trying to placate his grandson. Heaven help her, she wasn't hinting that she'd like to enter into a marriage contract. It was the last thing she wanted.

She could just imagine what her friends would say if she declared that she was marrying Ross Dufrais but she wasn't going to sleep with him, although she did have to promise that there'd be no other men in her life.

What a farce! What a ridiculous state of affairs! He couldn't be serious.

It would be sheer purgatory for whoever took the job because—and there was no denying it—he was one hell of a sexy man. Ignoring his gauntness, the weariness that encompassed him, it was easy to see what he'd used to be like. What he would be like again once he had got over his wife's death.

His eyes were fantastic: deep, dark pools that you could drown in, that would melt any susceptible girl on the spot. And his mouth, wide, generous, chiselled like the rest of his face, was entirely sensuous. She could imagine him kissing her, could imagine those sexy lips on hers, could...

'Is something wrong?' It was a harsh question.

Unaware that she'd been staring, Nicole jerked back to the present. 'No, no, of course not.' She felt her face flush. How stupid! This man wasn't in the least interested in her, or any woman for that matter, so why was she indulging in such fantasies?

'Were you wishing that you'd never come here?'

'I was thinking what a darling little boy your grandson is,' she lied.

'Aaron, yes.' His face softened, lost some of its gauntness. 'He means everything to me.'

More than a new wife ever could. It was implied, though not spoken. Nicole knew it was time for her to go, and yet she hadn't got the whole story. There were still gaps that needed to be filled. Where was Aaron's father, for instance?

'How did your wife and daughter die?' she asked with great daring.

It was as though a mask had been drawn over his face, skin stretched tightly over a fleshless skull. 'I have no wish to discuss it,' he said tersely. His eyes were lifeless, no longer darkly mysterious but cold, bottomless caverns.

'Then I think there's nothing further to keep me here,' she said, and rose to her feet. It was a pity she would never know the whole story.

'You don't want the job?'

Nicole frowned at the unexpected question. 'What do you mean?'

'I was about to offer it to you.'

'You were?' she asked in astonishment. 'Aren't there other applicants?'

'I haven't the time or inclination to see anyone else,' he answered with a dismissive lift of his broad shoulders. 'Do you want the job or don't you?'

CHAPTER TWO

ROSS'S offer was not the most persuasive, thought Nicole, and she was on the verge of declining when Aaron came running back into the room. 'Grandpa, come quickly. It's Tilda.'

Nicole was ignored as Ross strode out, Aaron clutching his hand and trotting beside him. 'What's wrong with her, Aaron?' she heard Ross ask.

'She says she needs the doctor. Will she have to go to hospital again? Is she going to die like my...?'

Nicole heard no more but it wasn't difficult to imagine what was going through the little fellow's mind. Ought she to follow? Ought she to offer help? Or should she quietly slip away?

Even while she was debating Aaron returned. 'Grandpa says will you look after me?'

He looked so small and trusting, his face upturned to hers, his dark eyes wide and so very much like his grandfather's. He was going to be one very big heart-throb when he grew up.

Nicole dropped to her knees and gave him a big hug. 'Of course I will. Shall we go and look at your new cars?'

He nodded and happily led the way upstairs to his bedroom. It was filled with toys—stacked on shelves, piled in boxes, taking every available space—so many that she couldn't believe he had new ones too. 'Gosh, who bought you all these?'

Aaron smiled broadly. 'Grandpa.'

'He's very good to you.'

In fact it looked as though he spoilt him rotten.

18

'I love Grandpa.'

'How about Daddy?' It was naughty asking questions of the child which she hadn't dared ask Ross, but she wanted some answers.

'I don't have no daddy.' It was said quite matter-of-factly.

'You've never had a daddy?'

Aaron shook his head. 'Look at my new cars.'

So Ross's daughter had had a child out of wedlock and the father was nowhere to be seen! And this poor little chappie now had no one but his grandfather and Tilda to look after him. And Tilda was very ill. No wonder Ross looked at the end of his tether.

A short time later she heard a car pull up outside, and then another vehicle, and when she looked out of the window it was an ambulance. As she didn't want to alarm Aaron she went back to playing with him on the floor. The carpet had roads and houses and parking areas and railway lines woven into it, and they were having a fine game when Ross came to find them.

He looked first at Aaron, absorbed in backing his new Porsche into a driveway, and then at Nicole. He beckoned her outside.

'I have to accompany Tilda to the hospital,' he said gravely.

Nicole nodded. 'I saw the ambulance—but I didn't tell Aaron; I didn't want to worry him.'

'That's good. Thank you,' he said gratefully. 'And now I have another favour to ask. Could you possibly stay with him until I get back?'

'Of course,' said Nicole at once.

'I'm sorry to encumber you with my grandson, but—'

'Think nothing of it,' she said. 'I'll stay for however long is necessary. May I use the phone to let my flatmates know where I am?' They would be eagerly awaiting the outcome of the interview and might fear she'd been abducted or something equally as sinister if she didn't arrive home.

'Of course. Perhaps you'll tell Aaron once I've gone, otherwise he'll clamour to come with me.'

It wasn't until she heard the ambulance pull away that Nicole marvelled at Ross trusting her so much that he was prepared to leave his beloved grandson with a complete stranger. Even leaving her in his house was taking a risk. He knew nothing about her. She could rob him, she could trash the place, she could kidnap Aaron. Anything.

A quarter of an hour passed before Aaron, tired of playing, announced that he was going to find his grandfather.

'Aaron—' Nicole, still kneeling on the floor, looked at him seriously '—Tilda's been taken to hospital. Grandpa's gone with her. How about if I get you ready for bed and then we'll look at your books until he returns?'

'I want my grandpa.' Tears filled the little boy's eyes and he stamped his foot, and his face started to go red.

'Aaron, sweetheart, he won't be long.' Nicole gathered him to her. 'And he'll be really pleased with you if you're in your pyjamas when he comes back.'

He struggled free and his little eyes glared at her. 'I want my grandpa.'

'I know,' she said soothingly, 'but Tilda needs him. You like Grandpa with you when you're ill, don't you?'

His lips were mutinously tight, but he gave a tiny nod.

'So don't be angry with him because he's gone with Tilda. He won't be long, I promise.'

Gradually Aaron accepted the inevitable, and when Ross did return he was sitting up in bed, bathed and in his pyjamas, and Nicole was reading him his favourite story.

'I apologise for leaving you to cope with Aaron,' he said, once he had kissed his grandson goodnight and assured him that Tilda would be home soon. 'I don't know what I'd have done if you hadn't been here.'

'You'd have taken him with you,' she assured him, 'or called in a neighbour.'

He nodded. 'I guess so. Do you realise you've worked wonders with him? He hates going to bed. How did you do it?' He dragged his hand tiredly through his hair as he spoke.

She shrugged. 'I'm used to my sister's children. All it took was a little persuasion.'

'And the rest,' he said drily. 'I know what Aaron's like. Can I offer you a drink? A G&T, wine, whisky, brandy? Anything?'

'I'm driving,' Nicole reminded him with a wry smile. 'But I could murder a coffee. How's Tilda?'

'She's comfortable. Worried to death about me leaving Aaron. I assured her you'd look after him well.'

Nicole's eyes widened. 'You told her about me?'

'Of course.'

'She knows you advertised for a wife?' She was incredulous.

'Goodness, no!' he said with a self-conscious laugh. 'I simply said you were my new girlfriend. She's longing to meet you.'

Oh, Lord! She was getting deeper and deeper into this. If she wasn't careful she'd end up taking the job—and that wasn't in her plan of things at all.

'Didn't it occur to you that she might answer the phone and find out?'

He gave a faint shrug. 'She never does these days; her hearing isn't so good.'

'Well, I hope you didn't promise to take me to see her,' Nicole protested furiously. 'This is dreadful. I'm not sure that I'm ready for any of this.'

A dark frown savaged his brow. The harshness was back. 'So why are you here?'

Nicole lifted one slender shoulder. 'I don't really know.'

What else could she say? Certainly not that she planned to write an article about him, about the extraordinary fact that he'd advertised for a wife.

And then, surprisingly, he smiled, and his whole attitude changed again. 'Aaron seems to have taken a liking to you.'

'He's a sweet child, very lovable.' She followed him into the kitchen, where he picked up the kettle and turned to the tap to fill it.

'Will you consider the job?' His back was to her as he asked the question but Nicole sensed that her answer was important to him.

'It's strange hearing you say "job" when you mean be a wife. In fact it's the weirdest proposal I've ever had.'

He turned to look at her then, leaning back against the counter in the neat oak kitchen, his eyes narrowing sharply on her face. 'There've been others?'

Nicole shrugged. 'One, actually, and that wasn't romantic either. He wanted to marry me for economic reasons. He wanted me to chuck my friends out of the flat so that he could move in.'

'And you didn't love him enough to do that?'

'No.'

'Will you marry me without love?'

Nicole was a long time in answering. She could feel herself getting pushed into a corner and she couldn't understand why she wasn't fighting her way out. The longer she dallied the harder it would be, the more convinced Ross would become that she'd accept. So why was she hesitating? 'I'd like to know why you're doing it,' she said eventually.

'I've told you—to make Tilda happy.'

She frowned. It sounded the weakest of arguments.

'And Aaron, of course.'

'And do you really think it will make any difference to

him whether you're married or not?' she asked incredulously.

'Aaron needs a mother figure for a while. Grandmother, actually,' he admitted wryly, 'but who's worrying? Tilda's always done her best, and she likes to think that she can still cope. There are times when you wouldn't know there's anything wrong with her—but there was an incident recently that I wouldn't like repeated. I have to think of Aaron. I have to put his safety first.'

'What happened?'

His mouth twisted wryly. 'She fell asleep in the garden and Aaron wandered off. We had a full-scale police search. He was missing for hours. I feared the worst.'

'But he was found safely?'

'Yes,' he admitted with a sheepish grimace. 'In Tilda's bed, would you believe? The duvet was crumpled and he's such a tiny mite you couldn't tell he was there.'

Nicole tried not to smile. Ross must have felt such a fool. 'At least he came to no harm,' she said quietly.

'But he might have done,' insisted Ross. 'And Tilda's not going to get any better. I can't tell her, though, that she's no longer capable. She's my mother's sister, and she brought me up when my parents died—I don't want to hurt her feelings.'

'Hence the fake wife?'

He nodded briefly, uncomfortably, and turned his attention back to the kettle. 'Do you mind instant?'

'It's all I drink,' she said. 'Preferably decaf.'

'Sugar? Milk?'

'Just milk, thanks. What was your wife like?' The question popped out before she could stop it. Diplomacy wasn't one of her strong points. If she thought something she usually said it, and if people didn't like it it was too bad.

Ross stilled, and at first she thought he wasn't going to answer. But finally he spoke and his voice was very quiet.

'She was pretty, vivacious, tactful, a good mother—a good everything, in fact. I miss her like hell.' The hurt was almost tangible.

'I'm sorry I asked,' she said faintly. 'I can see how difficult it is for you to talk about her.'

'No!' He swung back to look at her, pain sharply etched into his face. 'Don't apologise. It's a perfectly normal question. Actually it might be a relief to talk. I've buried my head in the sand for too long.'

Oh, God! Did she really want a conversation about his dead wife?

The phone rang. It was the hospital. Matilda was demanding her own nightdress and toiletries.

'I'll have to take them,' he said, 'or she'll drive the nurses crazy. Can I possibly ask you to stay a while longer and keep an ear open for Aaron? I promise I won't be long.'

'I could take them for you if you like,' she offered, feeling herself being wedged more deeply into the corner. 'I could drop them off on my way home.'

Ross shook his head. 'She won't rest unless I give them to her personally. I'm sorry I'm imposing on your time again.'

Nicole spread her hands and pulled a wry face. 'I'll wait.'

The corners of his mouth lifted in a vague smile of thanks, but it was easy to see that he was worried about his aunt. 'Help yourself to biscuits or something with your coffee. Watch the TV, read a magazine. Make yourself at home.' He was already heading out of the door.

It was a strange feeling, being left entirely to herself in Ross's house. Now that Aaron was asleep there was nothing to occupy her. She took her coffee through to the sitting room and sat looking out at the almost dark sky. When she'd finished her drink she wandered around the room, looking at the various pictures and ornaments, hoping to find some sort of clue as to what his wife had been like.

There was not a single photograph of her, which she found very odd. In fact no photographs at all. The cottage was actually quite impersonal, and she wondered how long he'd lived here.

Perhaps he'd moved after his wife and daughter had died. What a tragedy that was! Perhaps they'd never lived here at all. Perhaps he'd started a new life. And now he wanted another wife, but with no emotional commitment because he had no intention of ever falling in love again.

Had there been any other women in the last twelve months? It was a long time to remain celibate. He didn't have to love a woman to bed her. There'd be plenty who'd be only too willing to jump into bed with such a gloriously sexy man. Perhaps he had women-friends who satisfied his appetite but none who were interested in looking after his aunt and son?

When she'd phoned her friends earlier they'd expressed disbelief that Ross Dufrais had left her alone in the house with his son. They'd said he must fancy her and she'd better watch out or she'd end up as his wife after all.

She mused on what it would be like to be married to this handsome man, to be seen by all as his blissful bride, whereas in fact she'd be nothing more than a skivvy. And yet, as she sat there, the idea of becoming Mrs Ross Dufrais did not seem so bad.

She needed a job; he was offering one—a well-paid one. She wouldn't need to spend a penny; all she earned could go straight into the bank. At the end of it she'd have a very healthy balance. Was that worth giving him a few months of her life?

And apart from that she did feel sorry for him. What sort of work he did she didn't know, but it obviously took him out of the house for a great deal of each day. It must worry him to death, leaving Aaron with Tilda now that she was ill. He was such a darling little boy, so lovable, so trusting. He'd taken to her immediately—as she had to him.

The more she sat and thought about it the more the idea appealed. Treat it as a job. Don't think of him as a man, a damned sexy man. Ignore that altogether. Think of Aaron, think of living in this lovely cottage overlooking the sea. It would be sheer heaven compared to the flat with its view of ugly rooftops.

She was still thinking when Ross returned.

'I cannot believe that I've actually committed myself.' Ross shook his dark head as he looked at his business partner. 'This has to be the craziest thing I've ever done.'

Mark grinned. 'I think it was a stroke of genius putting that advertisement in.'

'Do you?' Ross glared at his long-time friend. 'I planned to find a wife in my own time in my own way—without your damned interference. You had no right doing it.'

'You needed shaking up, dear friend. We both agreed you needed a new woman in your life.'

'But not this way.'

Mark shrugged, completely unrepentant. 'What is done is done. Tell me what she's like. Is she beautiful or has she a face like the back of a bus? Has she a good figure or is she as fat as a pig?'

'Don't be derogatory, Mark. As a matter of fact she's very nice.'

'*Very nice!*' mimicked Mark. 'And what's that supposed to mean? Apple pie is "very nice". "Nice" doesn't describe anything, it has to be the most insipid word ever invented. I'll tell you what, why don't you invite me over for dinner this evening, and then I can see for myself what this wonder woman is like?'

Ross shook his head. 'Not a good plan, my friend. It's her first day; it wouldn't be fair.'

'Come off it, Ross. If I hadn't put that ad in you'd be in real trouble while Tilda's in hospital. Look how much time you had to take off when she was in before. You owe it to me.'

'I owe you nothing.' Ross rubbed the back of his neck. He'd had a sleepless night wondering whether he'd done the right thing. Right for Aaron, yes. And right for Tilda, because she found it difficult to cope. *But right for him?*

Marriage to a stranger!

Would it work? Was it too drastic a step to take? Why couldn't he simply employ Nicole as a glorified house-keeper?

Because, the answer came back, you're doing it for Matilda. She was the person he owed. She had put her own life on hold so that she could bring him up when his parents' lives had been cut tragically short. Her fiancé had walked out on her because of it, but she hadn't flinched from what she had seen as her duty. Unfortunately she'd never found another man.

And now it was her dearest wish to see her beloved Ross married again, and he'd decided that if he could make whatever time she had left happy it was the least he could do.

On returning from the hospital last night he'd been so tired that all he'd wanted to do was send Nicole home and go to bed. But he'd been instantly alert again when she had said quietly, 'I'll take the job.'

'You will?' he'd asked in genuine surprise. She'd seemed very much against such a hare-brained scheme, and he hadn't blamed her. He'd fully intended giving Mark another piece of his mind.

'If you're still offering?'

She hadn't looked too eager, and he'd wondered why she was saying yes. He supposed it was for the money. But that was all right because he had no intention of sleeping with her. Memories of Alison were still too strong. He didn't want to make love to anyone else. He didn't want to get involved again—and hurt again!

'Yes, Nicole,' he had said gratefully, 'the offer is still open. I promise you won't regret it.'

They'd spent almost an hour thrashing out details of the so called 'contract.' He wanted some kind of signed paper so that he wouldn't be left with a wife he didn't want at the end of it all. But, equally important, he wanted Nicole to feel that she was getting a fair deal.

He'd offered a more than generous salary and they'd agreed to review the position when necessary—it was impossible for the doctors to put a length of time on Matilda's life. How could you calculate something like that?

Nicole had agreed to start work straight away under the circumstances, although she wasn't going to move in until they were actually married. Aaron had been excited when she'd turned up this morning, and although Ross didn't foresee any problems he'd given Nicole his office telephone number just in case.

Several times he'd been tempted to phone, but on each occasion he'd had second thoughts. He had to trust her. He was about to put his life in her hands. Or was she putting hers in his? He wasn't quite sure.

He wasn't even sure why he'd invited her to come and see him, why he hadn't said the advertisement was a mistake and had done with it. Except that there'd been something in her voice that had made him want to see her, to see if she matched the husky tones that had instantly entranced him. And it was because he wanted to hear her voice again that he was tempted to phone her now. It was difficult concentrating on the mountain of paperwork on his desk.

'So when am I going to meet this *nice* woman?' persisted Mark. He was shorter than Ross, with a crop of thick fair hair and laughing blue eyes.

'At the wedding and not a moment before,' retorted Ross firmly. 'Look, we have heaps of work to get through. Let's forget this, shall we?'

'How can I forget such a significant event? I reckon you ought to pay me for the cost of that ad. I've done you a real favour.'

'Go to hell,' snarled Ross.

Mark laughed.

'Nicole! Nicole! Look at my picture.'

Aaron tugged at Nicole's blue sweater and she turned from preparing their sandwich lunch to look with interest at his crayon sketch.

'It's you,' he said. 'You and Grandpa.'

'And what am I wearing?' *It looked like a wedding dress!*

'You're getting married,' he said importantly.

It *was* a wedding dress! 'Is that what you think Grandpa and I are going to do?'.

He nodded emphatically. 'Tilda told me.'

Damn Tilda! She must have let her mind run riot the instant Ross had told her he had a girlfriend. 'And do you want me to be your new grandma?' God, it made her sound ancient, like a cosy grey-haired woman who baked cakes and sat knitting in front of the TV. Ugh!

When she'd told Terri and Marie that she was going to marry Ross Dufrais they'd thought she'd gone out of her head. 'But you were only supposed to be interviewing him,' Terri had said. 'Are you crazy? You know nothing about him. He could be a drug addict, a serial killer, anything.'

But when she'd told them how much he was going to pay her they had both changed their minds. And even wished that they'd answered the ad instead.

Ross had informed her that he would arrange a register office wedding for a week's time. Personally she couldn't see what the hurry was. 'Wouldn't it be simpler if I just moved in with you?' she asked.

But he shook his head. 'Tilda wouldn't approve. She has very strong principles. She believes in love at first sight as a matter of fact.'

'And is that what you let her think happened to us?' It was too appalling for words.

'I'm afraid so.'

'So when your aunt comes home she'll expect us to be a lovey-dovey couple?' Nicole couldn't keep the horror out of her voice. 'I don't think I like this game. And I'm quite sure you haven't stopped to consider the ramifications. You really are taking things too far.'

A glare from those magnificent dark eyes; a narrowing of those sensual lips. 'Since I'm going to marry you it's what she'll expect.'

'And I'm supposed to take part in it?' she sneered.

'Of course.' His shrug completely dismissed her argument. 'It's what I'm paying you for.'

'Well, damn you, Ross Dufrais,' she flung at him furiously. 'I'm not going to kiss and cuddle in front of your aunt for any amount of money.'

'Oh, I think you will,' he told her icily, his chin lifted, eyes narrowed. 'You're forgetting you've signed the contract.'

'Well, maybe I'll damn well *un*sign it.' She glared with equal fierceness.

'There's no going back.'

And she knew that he meant it.

'Nicole, I'm hungry.'

She was brought back to the present with a start.

Aaron pronounced her name Nickle and it made her smile. 'Our sandwiches are almost ready,' she said. 'Shall we take them outside?'

'To the beach?' His little face lit up.

'Maybe we'll go there afterwards,' she said gently. 'We'll sit on the lawn now. You go and spread the blanket.' Although it was the beginning of October they were experiencing an Indian summer and it was easily warm enough to sit out.

Nicole wondered, as they ate, whether she'd be expected to leave as soon as Ross came home. Or was she supposed to stay and eat with him, even cook their evening meal? It was something they hadn't discussed.

Even as she pondered the telephone rang. She ran inside to answer. 'About tonight,' Ross said, as though he'd honed in on her thoughts. 'I'm going to the hospital before I come home. Could you stay and put Aaron to bed? And then perhaps you'll share a meal with me?'

When she was a long time in answering he added, 'Of course. You've made other plans. Selfish of me! Forget it; I'll be home at six.'

'No, it's all right,' she said then. She'd been thinking that she might as well move in straight away if this sort of thing was going to happen often.

'Are you sure?'

'Yes, I'm sure.' She had nothing else to do, so why not?

'I shouldn't be too late. How's Aaron? Is he behaving himself?'

'He's fine. Do you want to speak to him?'

'If he's there.'

The boy had followed her into the house and was standing right beside her. She gave him the phone and smiled as he chatted to his grandfather, telling him in such a grown-up way what they were doing and what they were planning to do.

Later they went exploring. The receding tide had left a wide expanse of sand where the derelict boats sat drunkenly, and on either side of the estuary were lots of little rock pools which Aaron searched diligently for stranded crabs.

When they got home she cooked the young boy's supper and then bathed him and put him to bed. He was so tired after his busy afternoon that he didn't argue. And when Ross arrived she had their meal almost ready.

It didn't feel quite right, cooking in someone else's kitchen, providing food for a man she'd met only the day before, but who—in a few days' time—would be her husband!

And when they sat down for their meal he told her that the plans for their wedding were complete. 'Wednesday at ten-thirty.' He said it as matter-of-factly as if it was an appointment at the dentist. No emotion, nothing. A sheer dead-pan expression.

Nevertheless it sent a flurry of sensation through Nicole's stomach and she found it difficult to look at him, shuffling her chicken around the plate, prodding it with her fork.'

'I can assure you it's dead,' he said drily.

She did manage to look at Ross then, and he was smiling. Though it didn't reach his eyes. But she smiled back anyway.

'It bothers you, does it, this arrangement?' he asked.

Nicole pulled a face. 'I'd be lying if I said no.'

'So why did you answer the advert?'

'Curiosity, I guess.'

Eyebrows rose. 'Well, I for one am glad you were curious. I assure you that you've no cause for concern. It's just a job. You have nothing to fear from me. And Aaron, well, he loves you already. I think it should work very well.'

Nicole slowly nodded. She wished she had his confidence. It wasn't looking after his grandson and the house that worried her. It was the thought of pretending to be in love with him when the occasion demanded it—and once

Matilda was out of hospital then those occasions would be far too frequent.

'You'll need a new outfit for the wedding. I'll foot the bill, naturally. And then—'

'You don't have to do that,' Nicole cut in swiftly. It wasn't as though it was a *real* wedding. 'I have something I can wear. There's no point in you—'

It was Ross's turn to interrupt. 'There is every point. I don't want my new bride to look anything but stunning.'

Nicole shrugged her slender shoulders. So, let him spend his money. He seemed to have more of it than sense. 'What do you do for a living?' As usual she asked the question the instant it came into her head.

He frowned. 'I thought we were discussing the wedding?'

'What is there to discuss? You seem to have thought of everything.'

'I'm sorry the subject bores you.' His voice suddenly became distant.

'It's not that,' Nicole said quickly. 'But the way I see it, it would be a complete waste of money to buy a new outfit for what is after all only play-acting. I have a perfectly good suit that I bought for a cousin's wedding last year which will do the job.'

'And the way I see it,' he returned, a faint frown of annoyance on his brow, 'I want my wife to wear the customary new outfit.'

They were arguing, thought Nicole. Already! And over something so trivial! Did it augur well for the future? For the unprecedented months that lay ahead? She shrugged indifferently. 'It's your decision. You're calling the tune. Is there a lesson to be learned here? Do you always have your own way?'

He looked at her with one eyebrow quirked, his head to

one side. 'I don't think that question deserves an answer,
do you?'

It was a quiet rebuke, and, recalling how much he'd already been hurt, Nicole gave herself an inward shake. This
was no way to start. 'I'm sorry.'

'I suggest you finish your dinner.'

And then go home, were the unspoken words. Nicole
forced down the chicken and the salad, and the potato cro-
quettes she'd prepared with such care, and then pushed her
chair away from the kitchen table. 'Pudding?' she asked
abruptly.

'You've made one?'

'Just baked apples with apricot purée.'

'My favourite! How did you know?'

'It's mine too,' she said with a faint wry smile.

'So we do have something in common?'

Nicole felt faintly better as she arranged the apples on a
plate and took it to the table with a dish of clotted cream.
Ross looked as though he hadn't been eating well for a
long time, so it was satisfying seeing him tuck into her
cooking with such relish.

But when she got home and her friends asked how her
day had gone, she realised that her satisfaction hadn't come
from seeing him eat, but—disturbingly—from spending
time with him!

CHAPTER THREE

NICOLE was up early the next morning, rising with the dawn and jogging through the almost empty streets. Back at the flat she took a shower, drank two cups of coffee, and before her friends had even raised their heads from their pillows she set off for work.

Work! It could hardly be called that when it was going to be such a pleasure spending time with Ross. Except, she reminded herself, he would be out at work for the biggest part of each day. She might not see very much of him.

Discovering how much pleasure she'd felt in his company had been a considerable shock. It was something she hadn't expected, hadn't anticipated. He was an attractive man, yes, but no more so than a lot of other men she'd met—and she hadn't felt any leaping responses to them. So why now? What did it mean?

When she drew up in front of the cottage Ross greeted her at the door. He was wearing a navy suit and crisp white shirt with a neatly patterned silk tie. Her heart gave an unexpected lurch. He looked gorgeous. But no time for thinking about that.

'Nicole, you're a lifesaver,' he said. 'You must be telepathic. I rang the flat but was told you weren't there. I think I woke your friends. I'm needed at the hospital. I shall go straight to work afterwards. Aaron's still asleep. Will you—?'

She didn't let him finish. 'Of course. What's wrong with your aunt? Is she worse?'

'I'm not sure. They wouldn't tell me over the phone.'

35

There were fresh lines of tiredness on his face, as though he hadn't slept much, and now this additional worry.

'I hope it's not serious,' she said. 'Don't fret about Aaron; I'll stay for however long is necessary.'

'Nicole?'

'Yes?' There was something about the way he said her name that made her look at him warily.

'Would it be too big an imposition to ask you to move in straight away? I didn't plan this to happen, but with Tilda in hospital it's made things very difficult as far as Aaron's concerned.'

Nicole ignored the disturbing leap of her senses, inclining her head and looking at him with the seriousness she felt the occasion demanded. 'Of course. Your grandson's needs must come first.'

'I'll make it up to you.'

'There's no need.' She shook her head firmly. 'I adore him. He's sweet, he's intelligent, he's funny, he's well-behaved. It's not a problem. I don't know why you're worrying. You can rely on me any time.' She was talking too much, she knew, and yet she couldn't seem to stop. 'I love kids anyway, so it's not a chore; it's not like a real job. I—'

He smiled at last, a smile that softened his features and made him look less tired—and more gorgeous! 'OK, Nicole, you've made your point. Thank you. I'm leaving now. Expect me when you see me.'

She nodded. 'I'll take Aaron to the flat with me to pick up my stuff, if that's all right?'

'What? Oh, yes, of course.' His mind was already on other things.

The day was long, but there was plenty to do and Aaron was a joy to be with. She even managed to convince herself that the attraction she'd thought she felt for Ross was a figment of her imagination. Except that when he returned she experienced a further kick of awareness and it disturbed her. It was something that wasn't allowed to go with the job.

The trouble was he was so incredibly sexy and masculine and handsome that no woman in her right mind would be immune to him for long. It was a matter of ignoring her feelings and acting with the decorum her position called for.

'How's your aunt?' she asked.

'She's all right. It wasn't a crisis over her health—she wanted to ask me something. That woman has to be the most demanding person I know.' But he didn't sound cross.

Ross spent over an hour with his grandson and Nicole watched the two dark heads huddled together as they lay on the floor playing racing cars. It was a passion of Aaron's. He wanted to be a racing car driver when he grew up.

They both had the same strong profile, one almost harsh, the other soft and untouched by the ravages of time. It was uncanny how alike they were, dark hair constantly falling over their foreheads to be pushed back by an impatient hand. More like father and son than grandfather and grandson. The Dufrais genes were obviously strong.

Bathtime came and Ross took over, but he invited Nicole to join them. She was entranced as this big strong man bathed his small grandson: hands gentle as they soaped, careful, thorough, loving—and then he found Aaron's ticklish spot on the soles of his feet and the bathroom floor was soaked as the two of them convulsed with laughter.

But soon Aaron was in bed and asleep and they were alone. Nicole felt faintly uncomfortable. It was the first time she'd shared a house with a man.

It would be different if they were lovers; there'd be no atmosphere between them. They'd laugh and tease; they'd make love. There'd be no inhibitions. This was much more difficult. Here she had to tread carefully. This was a business relationship and she mustn't forget it, she mustn't let him see by even the flutter of an eyelash that she was attracted to him.

And because of her growing feelings the idea of writing an article about a man who'd advertised for a wife didn't seem such a good one after all. Not when she was in danger of becoming personally involved.

For their supper she'd cooked beef Bourguignon. She had no idea of his tastes, but she'd found the beef in the fridge and it had seemed a good way of using it.

'You're a good cook,' he praised as they sat facing each other across the kitchen table. Nicole had toyed with the idea of laying the table in the dining room, but good sense had prevailed. She didn't want him to think she was out to impress, or that eating together meant anything to her.

She'd thought it would be more casual and relaxed in the kitchen—but it wasn't. She was too aware of him, of the long outstretched legs that were so close to her own, of those sensual lips and the dark, dark eyes that set every one of her nerve-ends dancing.

Although she tried not to look at him it was as if a magnetic force compelled her eyes to meet his. And each time they did she would dart them quickly away again.

'Thank you,' she said. 'My mother taught me. She thought it an important accomplishment.'

'Good for your mother. She did an excellent job.'

'She taught cookery at a college in Exeter.'

'She still lives nearby?'

Nicole shook her head. 'No. She's in Canada now, and my father's in Scotland.'

'They're divorced?'

'I'm afraid so.' It had been a very sad time when they'd split up, but she'd been old enough to accept it without any rancour.

'Do you see them often?'

'Not as much as I'd like.' And she deliberately changed the subject. 'Tell me about you. You still haven't told me what you do for a living.'

'I guess we haven't had time to talk.' He leaned back in his chair, his knife and fork laid to rest for a moment. 'I run a restaurant. Well, several actually,' he admitted with a faint wry smile.

'Really?' she asked with interest. 'Where? Which ones? Would I know them?'

'You might. There's Rails in Bude, Sandpipers in St Ives, Plovers in Newquay.'

'Goodness, yes!' she exclaimed excitedly. 'They're top restaurants.' And he owned them! 'I've been to Rails, but only on very special occasions. I can't afford their prices every day.'

'My standards are high, I know,' he admitted. 'But it's proved worthwhile.'

'I'm impressed.'

'There are others too, and I'm hoping to expand even further, move into other parts of the country. I think we've pretty well saturated Cornwall.'

Goodness! He had to be worth a small fortune, and yet he lived in this modest cottage. Why? But she knew she didn't dare ask. 'They must keep you very busy?' she said instead.

'I have a partner who looks after the financial side of things—I prefer to be in on the action—but, yes, we are busy. More so in the summer months, naturally, but even so we do a steady trade all year round.'

'How did you start?' She was fascinated by this glimpse into his life and wanted to know more.

'With a little café right here in St Meek. I moved from the Midlands when my daughter was small. It was hard work. I did all my own cooking, Alison waited on tables,

Matilda looked after Tara. But it paid off. Within two years I was able to expand.'

'And now you're able to sit back and reap the rewards?'

There were no rewards as far as Ross was concerned. The pleasure had gone out of it. He carried on for Aaron's sake, because one day the business would be his.

Dammit, why had he walked away scot-free when Alison and Tara had been killed? Would he ever forgive himself?

Loving someone was too painful an emotion. Every single person he'd loved had died at an early age. Both sets of grandparents when he was very young. Then his parents when he was barely a teenager. It had left his world empty.

His aunt Matilda had moved in, but it hadn't been the same, and then when he was sixteen he'd met Alison. She had been beautiful, she had been fun, she had been clever. He'd fallen deeply in love with her and she with him. They'd married three months later, against his aunt's wishes—against everyone's wishes, in fact—and nine months later baby Tara had been born.

He'd suddenly felt whole again. He'd had his own family and he'd worked hard for them, his life fulfilled—until that dreadful day. It would live in his mind for ever. It was obvious his destiny had been mapped out for him. It wasn't in the plan of things for him to love anyone. If he did they'd be torn from him.

He'd had twenty-one years with Alison, admittedly, but he had expected a lifetime, and now he'd made up his mind that he'd allow no one else to get beneath his skin. He was content with Aaron. His biggest fear was that something should happen to his grandson. Like the day he'd gone missing! He'd nearly had a heart attack.

So why, then, when he looked at Nicole sitting across the table from him, did he feel an urge to kiss her? He'd made up his mind that he'd let no emotions enter into this relationship. He'd even spelt it out to her.

He'd gained the impression that she was relieved, that she'd have walked out on him if he'd said he wanted more. It was the way she'd handled Aaron that had made him decide—and the fact that his grandson had instantly taken a liking to her.

Following Mark's ridiculous advert he'd had several phone calls, but if Nicole hadn't proved suitable he wouldn't have interviewed anyone else. It had proved too embarrassing. He'd have settled for a nanny and Matilda would have had to go on hoping.

At this moment he wished he *had* simply taken on some-one to look after Aaron. Nicole was extraordinarily beautiful. In the beginning he hadn't noticed; he'd been too busy making sure she was suitable for the rather unusual job. But now when he looked at her he saw her exquisite bone structure, her huge blue eyes—a dark, indigo-blue, a lovely colour—and her retroussé nose, and her wide, full-lipped mouth which was a natural rosy-red without any need for artifice.

In fact she never wore make-up, which was a plus as far as he was concerned. He liked her hair too. It was as sleek and as black as a raven's wing, even darker than his own, and it shone faintly blue in the sunlight. He'd never liked short hair on a woman, but Nicole's really did suit her. It framed her heart-shaped face in feather-like wisps and he found himself wanting to touch it.

As well as kiss her! Lord, what was happening to him?

'Are you all right, Ross?'

It was fortunate she spoke. It banished his unwelcome thoughts. 'Why do you ask?' It was the first time since Alison's death that he'd felt any sort of reaction to a woman and it stunned him. It was something he didn't want to happen, wouldn't let happen.

'You looked miles away.'

'I guess I was.'

'Would you like some time alone?'

Her unexpected question made him frown. 'Why do you ask?' He didn't realise how harshly he spoke.

Nicole shrugged. 'I don't know. You seem unhappy with my company.'

Was that what she thought? He'd been so used to being alone, to letting his thoughts wander at will, to not having to hide any of his torment, that he hadn't realised how transparent he was. He shook his head.

'Is it that you're having second thoughts? We don't have to go through with the wedding if you don't want to. You can tear up the contract. I'll still look after Aaron.'

It was a straw he almost clutched, but his aunt had been so pleased when he'd told her about Nicole, especially when he'd said they were getting married next week. It had given her a new lease of life and she was hoping to be out of hospital in time for the ceremony.

'I still want us to get married, Nicole,' he said quietly, firmly. 'I don't have a problem with that. Do you?' Perhaps if he put the ball in her court she'd stop questioning him.

'I'm getting used to the idea,' she said.

'I think that maybe tomorrow we should go out and buy your outfit.'

'We?' Her lovely eyes opened in shock. 'Isn't it customary for the bride to keep her wedding dress a secret from the groom?'

'This is hardly a normal wedding,' he declared irritably. What had prompted him to suggest they go together? It was an absurd idea.

'No, it's not,' she agreed, her tone equally as short. 'But I'd still prefer to go on my own, or at least with a girlfriend. Not with you.'

She made it sound abhorrent, and he wondered why

she'd agreed to become his wife. The main reason had to be for the money, but as he'd made it clear that there would be occasions when she'd need to pretend to be in love with him she must find him in some way tolerable.

Not that it should matter to him, and yet oddly it did. He wanted her to like him. He wanted her to—what did he want? The answer was not immediately apparent.

'Of course you want to go alone,' he acceded finally. 'But don't leave it until the last minute. In fact I'll take Aaron to see Tilda in the morning, so that you can do your shopping then. She keeps asking for him, so she'll be well pleased.'

And so Nicole went shopping for her wedding outfit— alone. But as she tried on dress after dress, suit after suit, she began to wish that she'd taken Ross up on his offer. She wanted to please him, and yet she didn't know what his tastes were.

In the end she settled for something classical and simple and hoped he'd approve. And when she got home his car was outside. Thank goodness she hadn't stopped to have lunch, as she'd been tempted to. He would be waiting to get back to work.

But a further surprise awaited her.

Aaron ran to her as soon as she opened the door. 'Nicole, Nicole, Tilda's home! Come and see.' And he caught her hand and dragged her, parcels as well, into the sitting room.

Matilda Rothersay was sitting in a high-backed chair near the window, her elbows on the wooden arms, her bony fingers supporting a number of fabulous heavy rings. She wore a fine crêpe purple dress with an amethyst brooch in the form of a lover's knot, and amethyst ear-studs, and her white hair was drawn back from her face in an immaculate French pleat.

Ross stood behind her with his hands on the back of the chair, and they both watched her intently.

Nicole found it unnerving to say the least, but she nevertheless dropped her bags and went towards Matilda, a ready smile on her lips. Remembering the woman's deafness, she spoke loudly. 'I'm so pleased you're home.'

'And I am pleased to meet you, my dear.' Grey eyes twinkled. 'Ross's told me all about you. It's the most wonderful surprise.' She held out both her hands and Nicole took them. They were cold and papery thin, but with surprising strength.

The woman looked down at their hands and frowned. 'You've no engagement ring! Ross, how very remiss of you.'

Nicole said immediately, 'It's been a whirlwind affair; we haven't had time for such niceties.'

Ross looked at her gratefully. 'She will have both on her wedding day.'

Matilda smiled. 'I'm really looking forward to that. I so desperately want to see my darling Ross happily married again. He's suff—'

'Don't start that!' Ross put a warning hand on his aunt's shoulder. 'This is a happy day. Nicole doesn't want to hear about such things.'

Matilda nodded. 'Very well, I'll talk to her later, when we're alone.'

Ross raised his eyes to the ceiling and Nicole guessed he was counting to ten. 'You won't talk about it at all, Tilda,' he said gently. 'It's in the past. The future is what's important.'

'Of course. Open the champagne, Ross. Time to celebrate.'

It was already nestling in ice, and now Ross opened the bottle of Louis Roederer Cristal with great aplomb and poured it into the waiting flutes.

'Can I have some?' piped up Aaron.

Tilda smiled and nodded, but Nicole noticed that a bottle of lemonade was close by.

'To Ross and Nicole,' said Tilda. 'May you find eternal happiness.'

Nicole saw Ross wince and guessed he was feeling guilty.

He lifted his glass. 'To you, Nicole.' And there was a wealth of meaning behind his words.

'And to you,' she said bravely.

And Aaron said seriously, 'To me.'

They all laughed and the tension was broken.

Ross sat down on the sofa and pulled Nicole beside him, tucking her into the curve of his arm, the warning dig of his fingers telling her that she'd better co-operate.

Her body unwittingly did more than that. Warm tingles ran along her thighs and through her stomach, condensing in the very heart of her. It was a shock to her entire system. It was all very well knowing that she was attracted, but to feel it with such fire was something else.

'Was your morning's shopping successful?' asked Ross.

'Oh, good Lord!' Nicole exclaimed. 'Everything's still in the bag. I must go and hang them up.' It was the very excuse she needed to escape him.

'Nonsense!' His arm tightened about her. 'Another half-hour won't hurt.'

'Ross tells me you've been shopping for your wedding outfit,' said Matilda. 'Am I going to be given a dress rehearsal? Or do I also have to wait until the Big Day?'

'I don't mind showing you,' said Nicole. 'But Ross definitely has to wait.'

He muttered something about the unfairness of it all, but his aunt merely laughed. 'There's a lot to be said for tradition, my boy. I'm glad Nicole has old-fashioned values. Tell me, Nicole, who are you inviting from your side?'

Nicole hadn't given it any thought. It wasn't as if it was a real wedding. She lifted her shoulders in a faintly apologetic shrug.

'Just two friends, I'm afraid. My parents are too far away and my sister's extremely pregnant with her fourth child. She's not going anywhere at the moment.'

'No aunts and uncles or cousins?'

'None who could come at such short notice,' she said. In actual fact she wasn't telling anyone. What was the point when it would be dissolved so quickly? They wouldn't understand what she was doing, they'd tell her she was a fool, and, well, maybe she was, but she wanted to help Ross out. And besides, she'd have a nice healthy bank balance at the end of it.

Not that she was thinking of her financial gain at this precise moment. Her tell-tale pulses were still having a ball.

'That's such a pity,' said Matilda. 'But still, I suppose a quiet, private gathering is as much as Ross needs. He had all the razzmatazz he wanted when he married Alison.'

Nicole felt the sudden tension in him. Matilda ought to know better than to bring up his beloved first wife.

She glanced at him and he squeezed her hand. 'The quieter the better,' he said. 'Mark's coming; he's the only one. I don't want any fuss, Tilda, so don't go planning anything behind my back or I'll be very cross.'

'Would I?' she asked. 'You're forgetting I'm a sick woman.'

'Ah!' he said. 'Of course. You couldn't possibly entertain any devious thoughts, could you?'

Nicole loved the gentle repartee between these two. It spoke a thousand words. And the fact that he was prepared to marry a complete stranger to make his aunt happy said another thousand. He was the most caring man she'd ever met, and Alison had been a very lucky woman, a very lucky woman indeed.

After a light lunch of vegetable soup and crusty bread, followed by fresh fruit, Ross left for his office. Aaron was tucked up in bed for his afternoon nap, and Matilda invited Nicole to come and sit with her.

'I want to hear all about how you met,' she said. 'Ross's such a dark horse; he never even told me had a girlfriend. And now here you are getting married. He said it was love at first sight. Is that right?'

Nicole had been expecting this, but even so was not prepared. She gave a wistful smile and a faint sigh. 'I guess so.'

The woman nodded, satisfied. 'I fell in love with my Tom at first sight. But it was not to be.' A moment's reflection, and then a shake of her head as she dismissed her thoughts. 'So tell me all about it. How did you meet my handsome nephew?'

'Didn't he tell you?'

'Not a word.'

So it was up to her to make up a convincing story! Nicole smiled faintly. 'I answered a job advertisement he'd put in the local paper.' At least that was the truth.

'Really?' Matilda's eyes lit up. 'And did he give you the job?'

'He did offer it to me.'

'Except that other things got in the way?' suggested Matilda with a delighted smile. 'Isn't it wonderful the way love can just hit you when you're least expecting it? Isn't it an amazing feeling? Don't you just burn up inside? I'm so pleased for you both. It's a dream come true. Poor Ross, he's suffered so; it's good to see him happy again. He told you about Alison, of course?'

Nicole nodded.

'She was a lovely girl—but so are you, dear child. And I know, I can feel it in my bones, that you're right for each other.' She closed her eyes and nodded. 'So very right.'

'Are you tired, Mrs Rothersay?'

'Please, call me Tilda. Everyone does. And, yes, I think I could do with a rest. Would you mind helping me to my room?

'Do you know, Nicole?' said the woman a few minutes later as she lay down on her bed. 'I'm the happiest woman alive. But do you know what will make me even happier?'

Nicole hadn't the faintest idea.

'For Ross to start another family.'

Heavens! thought Nicole, don't say that.

'I know there's Aaron, and Ross loves him dearly, but it's not like he's his own son. He doted on Tara. Another little girl would make him so happy. Please, Nicole, don't keep him waiting too long.'

CHAPTER FOUR

'WAKEY, wakey!'

Nicole forced open heavy eyelids and saw through a sleep-induced haze the smiling faces of her two flatmates.

'Time to rise and shine. Breakfast awaits the blushing bride.'

Nicole forced her eyes to operate properly. 'What time is it?'

'Seven o'clock.'

'It's still dark,' she grumbled. 'It can't be that time.' And she pulled the quilt over her head.

'It's raining,' said Marie, snatching it back again. 'That's why it's not light yet, but it's getting there. Come on, sit up. Breakfast in bed today.'

Reluctantly Nicole pushed herself up. Her pillows were plumped behind her back, and a tray was placed in front of her. She blinked. Not bacon and egg, not toast and marmalade, not cornflakes—but champagne and strawberries! 'What sort of a breakfast is this?' she asked, her eyes wide.

'A very decadent one,' Terri informed her. 'And you'd better enjoy it.'

'Are you joining me?'

'You bet.'

'I don't think I want to go through with this,' said Nicole as she bit into one of the fruits.

'With what? The breakfast?' asked Marie.

'The wedding, stupid. I've decided it's not a good idea.' Especially not with Tilda wanting them to produce a baby post-haste. She hadn't told Ross what his aunt had said, but guessed that he'd had the same sort of lecture.

'Not a good idea when you're talking mega-bucks,' declared Marie. 'You have to be crazy, dear friend. A clear case of wedding day nerves.'

'This is not a normal wedding,' Nicole reminded her.

'Do you like the guy?' asked Terri.

Did she like him? For the last six days she'd been fighting an incredible physical attraction. It was in danger of taking over her life. *That* was why marriage to Ross Dufrais would be a mistake not only a mistake, a disaster. She'd actually love to make babies with him, but the only interest he had in her was to keep his aunt happy; he'd made that very clear.

She'd managed to hide her feelings for six days, but for several months? Impossible. And once he knew how she felt it would create the most awful atmosphere. This was a marriage of expedience as far as he was concerned; feelings simply didn't enter into it.

'I said, do you like him?' Terri reminded her.

Nicole nodded slowly. 'Yes, I do.'

'You don't find him abhorrent or anything like that? It won't be too much of a penance being married to him?'

'I suppose not.'

'Then you have nothing to worry about, girl. I can't wait to meet him.'

'Me too,' added Marie. 'You never know, it might turn into a *real* marriage. Nudge, nudge wink, wink you know what I mean?'

'You're mad!' exclaimed Nicole, popping another sweet tasting strawberry into her mouth and washing it down with a swallow of champagne. 'Both of you.'

For Matilda's sake, to conform with tradition, she'd elected to spend her last night in her old room at the flat—which meant that Ross still hadn't seen her outfit, and nor would he see her before they met at the register office.

She had the feeling that he was as nervous about this

wedding as she was. In fact he hadn't mentioned it again until yesterday evening, when she'd told him about her sleeping arrangements.

'Is that necessary?' he'd asked with a frown. 'What if Aaron needs you? He's come to depend on you.'

'Then he'll have to make do with his grandpa, won't he?' she'd answered irritably. 'This is something I have to do, want to do, and you can't stop me.'

'You're not running out on me?'

Nicole had looked at him, her mouth dropping open in surprise. 'Is that what you think?'

Broad shoulders had risen and fallen again. 'Women have been known to change their mind.'

'Well, not this one,' she'd assured him. 'I signed your stupid bit of paper, didn't I? Which wasn't necessary, I can assure you. I never go back on my word.' Although she'd definitely been tempted—more than once—these last few days.

The enormity of what she was doing had suddenly hit her, and the fact that she fancied him something rotten had a whole lot to do with it. She could be in for a very miserable few months.

And what if Aunt Matilda lived for a whole while longer? What then? Had he thought that through? Would she be expected to carry on regardless? It didn't bear thinking about.

At ten o'clock she was ready.

At ten-fifteen the car came for her, the rain stopped and the sun came out.

At ten twenty-five she arrived at the register office.

At ten-thirty she became Mrs Ross Dufrais.

'Kiss the bride. Kiss the bride.'

Who said the words Nicole didn't know, but when Ross obliged, when he wrapped his arms around her, when his mouth took hers in a lifetime-long kiss, she felt as though she was going to pass out.

In the few days before the wedding they'd pretended, for Tilda's benefit. He'd held her hand, he'd embraced her, he'd even kissed her lightly, but nothing like this. This felt as though it was blowing the top off her head. It felt as though he meant it, even though she knew it was an act. She was careful not to respond, though it crucified her not to. It was the hardest thing she'd ever done.

And then, just as suddenly, she was free—dazed, but free. She looked at her friends, who gave her an instant thumbs-up, at Aaron, who looked adorable in a grown-up grey suit, at Tilda, who was grinning like a Cheshire cat, and at Mark, Ross's business partner, who had been eyeing her lasciviously ever since he'd set eyes on her. And finally she looked at Ross.

'Mrs Dufrais, you look stunning,' he said.

She looked more than stunning. She'd completely wowed him when they'd met outside. Her dove-grey silk suit skimmed her curves deliciously—and she seemed to be wearing nothing under the jacket. It was a thought that had tantalised him continuously throughout the ceremony.

She wore pale silk stockings on her long elegant legs and high-heeled buckskin shoes—it was strange he'd not noticed how long her legs were before—and on her head a ridiculous tiny froth of lilies and lace.

He'd heard Mark gasp and say, 'You call that *nice*? You must be blind, man. She's the sexiest creature I've ever seen. God, I envy you.'

And she did look gorgeous. Alison had been beautiful, but there was something about Nicole today that took his breath away. He felt flattered that she'd taken so much care because, in essence, it was a job, something she was getting paid to do. But because she was conscientious she was playing the part to perfection. Tilda was enormously pleased.

Ross had given Nicole a double string of pearls as a wedding gift—she'd balked at it and tried to say no, but he'd insisted—and he looked at them now in the vee of her jacket, just entering the delectable hollow between the swell of her breasts, and he felt a catch in his throat. Not for the first time Ross wondered whether he'd done the right thing.

'Time we made a move.' Mark's voice came over his shoulder.

'Nicole?' Ross held out his hand and she took it without the slightest hesitation, smiling into his face, looking for all the world like a bride truly in love. He was impressed. Well impressed. Because he knew that she had no feelings for him, that she suffered his touch for his aunt's sake. He'd felt her withdrawal time and time again, felt her stiffen, felt her rejection of him. But not today. She was superb. And he almost wished that this marriage was for real.

In the back of the wedding car on their return trip to the cottage he expected the bloom to leave her cheeks, the smile to fade, but, no, she still looked excited and happy.

'Thank you, Nicole,' he said softly.

She gave a faint frown. 'For what?'

'For making our wedding perfect.'

She hesitated, and he thought she was going to say that she'd enjoyed it, that it hadn't been the trial she'd expected, but instead she said, 'We fooled Tilda, didn't we?'

He was disappointed. It had all seemed so real, and he'd crazily wanted to keep it that way. 'So far, yes,' he agreed. 'But the day isn't over.'

'Nor the hundreds of days ahead,' she reminded him, and he thought he heard resignation in her voice.

'Are you regretting it already?' he asked sharply. He didn't want her to feel remorse. He wanted her to enjoy her job. *Job!* God, how could marriage be a job? Marriage was a commitment. Marriage was a union of minds and bodies. Or it should be. He pressed fingers to his suddenly aching temples. What had he done?

'No, Ross, I don't regret it.' Her hand touched his arm, her lovely blue eyes looking into his. 'Are you all right? Do you have a headache?'

'Tension, I think,' he lied.

'You need a massage. Here, let me.' And she put her fingertips where his had been, gently circling and soothing and then stroking her fingers over his brow and his closed eyelids, and then back to massaging his temples again.

He inhaled the sweet feminine scent of her, and wanted this moment to go on for ever. She seemed to know exactly what to do, where to touch, how to calm. Liar! He wasn't in the least calm. Her touch excited, it aroused, it created an instant adrenalin rush. Thoughts that shouldn't be allowed surged in his head, desire that had lain dormant since Alison's death flared into life. He could stand it no longer. 'That's it, thank you. I feel much better now.' His tone was unconsciously sharp.

'Are you sure?' Nicole's husky voice that had entranced him from the beginning sounded even deeper and sexier—or was it his imagination?

'Yes—and, look, we're almost home.'

He'd decided on a quiet meal at the cottage rather than in a hotel, in case Tilda got tired and needed to rest. And he was glad they'd arrived because he didn't know how much longer he could endure this close proximity without giving himself away.

The caterer he'd hired had everything ready. Champagne flowed freely and the fresh salmon and venison were delicious. Nicole still looked excited and happy, and Mark's speech made it clear that if he'd met Nicole first she wouldn't have married Ross today.

And afterwards Mark seemed to spend an age talking to

her. Ross couldn't take his eyes off them. Was his friend homing in on Nicole, ready to pounce when the marriage ended?

'It looks as though Mark fancies your wife. You'll have to watch him.'

He turned to find Terri and Marie standing beside him, a wide grin on both their faces. He liked Nicole's friends; they were open, fun-loving girls, and he could imagine that Nicole must miss them very much. He made a mental note to tell her that she could invite them over any time she wished.

They were joking, but how close to the truth their words were. Mark had been knocked for six when he'd seen Nicole, and, dammit, if body language was anything to go by she looked as though she found him attractive too. He gritted his teeth as he watched them.

'I think I might just go and let him have it straight between the eyes,' he said, wondering as he grinned at them whether they knew the truth behind his marriage. He ought to have asked Nicole. Actually they hadn't talked very much at all. It was something he must remedy.

'Oooh, not a good idea,' said Marie. 'I should hate to see his blood splatter on Nicole's new suit. I know a better way.' She winked at Terri. 'He's a bit of all right is Mark; I'll go and chat him up myself.' And she sauntered across the room, turning on a brilliant white smile as she tapped the fair-haired man on the shoulder.

'Ross's one helluva lucky guy.'

'In what way?' Nicole looked up at Mark where he had perched himself on the arm of the settee beside her. For the first time since they became husband and wife Ross had left her side and Mark had dived straight in.

'Marrying a stunner like you.'

She lifted an eyebrow. 'Then I guess I'm lucky too, to

be marrying someone as handsome as Ross.' She glanced across at her new husband as he handed his aunt a drink.

'And to think I played a part in it.'

Nicole drew her delicate brows together. 'I beg your pardon? What are you talking about?'

'The advert.'

She still looked blank.

'Didn't Ross tell you?' His grin was voracious. 'I was the one who put it in. You have a lot to thank me for, dear lady. I think maybe I deserve a kiss.' He dipped his head, but Nicole adroitly slid sideways and stood up.

Ross had let Mark advertise! It didn't make sense. Why? And why hadn't he told her? What sort of a man was he to let someone else manipulate his life?

Mark didn't look in the least put out that she'd avoided his kiss, simply standing as well and carrying on the conversation. 'I knew it was time he had a wife, but I didn't expect such instant results—or that you'd be such a stunner. I was saying to Ross earlier that I wished I'd met you first. I suppose there's no hope for me?'

This man was beginning to annoy her. He was good-looking, he was a life-and-soul-of-the-party type and he was Ross's partner, so she couldn't afford to upset him, but he was definitely getting on her nerves.

'Not a cat in hell's chance. Sorry.' She gave him a brilliant smile to defuse her words and noticed that Ross had finished with his aunt and was now standing talking to Marie and Terri. Time for her to make a move.

But before she could do so Marie appeared at her side. 'I've come for a chat with this gorgeous man. Ross's waiting for you—panting for it, I wouldn't wonder. Said something about it's time you left for your honeymoon.'

Honeymoon! How could they, with Tilda and Aaron to look after?

She was frowning as she rejoined him. Terri had already

moved away to play with Aaron and yet another new car. 'I didn't know we were going away?' she asked abruptly. 'You never said.'

It was his turn to frown. 'Who told you that?

'Marie.'

'Well, Marie's guessing, but as a matter of fact, yes, I have made plans, and maybe it's time we went.'

'But we can't. Aaron, your aunt…'

'I've made arrangements for them to be looked after.'

More plans without her! 'I haven't packed,' she protested.

'That's all right; I've packed for you.'

Packed for her! How dared he? But she let that go for the moment. 'But we can't go on honeymoon; this isn't a proper marriage.' She was becoming more and more agitated.

'No one else knows that. We're going whether you like it or not.'

His voice brooked no refusal but Nicole wasn't happy. She was being employed to look after his grandson and aunt, not go holidaying with him. It was ludicrous, entirely unnecessary. Nobody would think anything if they didn't go. They could always say they intended having a honeymoon later, when circumstances permitted.

'Does Tilda know?' she asked heatedly.

'Yes, and she's all for it.'

That would be about right. Tilda would want them to do everything properly. She thoroughly approved of their marriage. 'And Aaron?'

'Yes, he knows too.'

'Does he mind?'

Ross shrugged. 'At first he did, until I told him that a very kind lady with a boy his own age would be coming to stay, then he happily accepted the situation.'

'What lady?' she asked crossly.

'A qualified person. Don't worry. I got her from an agency.'

'So why not just employ *her*? Why did you have to marry *me*?' she demanded, even more angry now.

'My, my, we've been married only hours and already you're spoiling for a fight. This won't do, Nicole. It's not what I'm paying you for.'

She thought she saw a twinkle in his eye, but she was so enraged that she decided she must have imagined it. He wasn't amused; he was angry because she refused to see things from his point of view. Why couldn't he see them from hers?

A honeymoon, of all things! How were they supposed to spend that? Not in each other's beds, that was for sure. At each other's throats more likely.

'Where are we going on this *honeymoon*?' she asked, sarcasm dripping like ice off her tongue.

'You'll find out when we get there.'

Her chin came up. 'And what if I refuse to go with you?'

A warning flashed in his eyes; his spine straightened. 'If you do or say one thing to upset my aunt,' he bit out through clenched teeth, 'you'll regret it for the rest of your life.'

Nicole closed her eyes and shook her head, then snapped them open again when she felt his hand on her elbow. She was propelled across the room to where Matilda sat in her chair, taking everything in around her, nodding her head in satisfaction.

'Are you two lovebirds away now?' she asked. 'You mustn't miss your flight.'

So even his aunt knew where they were going! She wanted to spit in Ross's eye. But of course she didn't. She put on the front that had kept her going all day; she became the blushing bride again, bright eyes and loving smiles, her hand tucked into Ross's arm. 'You will be all right?'

'You can bet your bottom dollar on it,' said Matilda. 'I'm going to have a wonderful time imagining you two making babies.'

Nicole blushed furiously. Even Ross looked surprised, and his hand came over Nicole's when he felt her start to pull away. 'You're irrepressible, Tilda,' he scolded, even as he smiled. 'What am I going to do with you?'

'Go away and enjoy yourself,' she said, 'and then come back and tell me all about it.'

'I'll get our bags,' said Ross.

Left alone, Tilda said to Nicole, 'You're quite the most beautiful bride I've ever seen. Your love for Ross shines out of you. I am so happy.'

'I'm not sure we should go away and leave you, though,' Nicole began.

'Nonsense, girl. I shall be in perfectly safe hands. Ross's seen to all that. Now go and powder your nose, or whatever you need to do, then enjoy yourself with my blessing.'

How could she? Ross had really thrown her with his plans to go away. Whatever had possessed him? Tradition, she supposed. Keeping up the act for Tilda's benefit. Would tradition include a double bed? Would it include making love to her? Would she be able to resist him if he tried?

In the car, on the plane, Nicole remained silent, blanking out Ross's attempts at conversation, refusing to speak to him until in the end he gave up trying.

When they landed she had no idea where they were, and even when they got on to another plane, a small single-engined one, she didn't question him. It was a pointless exercise as far as she was concerned, a complete waste of time and money.

Their destination was an island, a lush green oasis in the middle of a sparkling blue ocean. A car awaited them and Ross drove to a beach house about two miles from the airstrip. The air was warm and sultry, the sky a deep hot blue, and the house built on stilts was enchanting—and completely isolated. A perfect place for honeymooners!

She waited until they were inside—bare wooden floors and knitted cotton rugs, shutters but no curtains, cane furniture, huge fans set in the ceiling: very minimalistic, very practical—and then said in a tiny tight voice that she didn't recognise as her own, 'What is the point in all of this?'

'The point,' said Ross as he moved through to the bedroom with their luggage—the *only* bedroom, Nicole noticed with sinking heart—'is that it is expected.'

'By whom?' she wanted to know. 'No one would have batted an eyelid if we hadn't come away. Everyone knows Tilda needs looking after, to say nothing of Aaron.'

'We need to get to know each other—properly.'

It was the way he said 'properly' that made her look at him, her blue eyes sparking points of fire.

'If you're suggesting what I think you are then you can forget it. It's not part of—'

'I'm simply suggesting that we talk,' he interrupted quietly—too quietly, suggesting controlled anger. 'Learn about each other. We know nothing at the moment and it's difficult to get time alone.'

Nicole sniffed indelicately. 'We could have done that in England. In any case I don't see the importance, so long as I do the job you're paying me for.'

He snorted savagely. 'If we're to convince my aunt, then it *is* important, extremely so. She's already asked me questions about you that I can't answer. But don't worry. I won't touch you, if that's your problem.'

It was almost as good as saying that he didn't *want* to touch her. Her chin lifted heroically. 'I never even thought about it,' she lied.

'No? You're saying that you hadn't even noticed that there's only one bedroom, one bed?' His eyes flicked from her, to it, and back again.

'I'd noticed.'

'At least it's king-sized,' he said with a certain amount of satisfaction.

That was what troubled her. It was big enough to share without them touching—theoretically. In practice? Doubtful. So who got the bed and who the uncomfortable-looking settee?

'Perhaps you'd like to unpack and take a shower while I fix us something to eat.'

'I'm not hungry.'

'A drink, then?'

She nodded.

'Champagne?'

'No, I've had enough of that for the moment. A soft drink, I think. Lime and lemon—something like that. Is this place well stocked?'

'It should be; I gave instructions.'

'You've been here before?'

'Yes.'

'Who does it belong to?'

'Me.'

That shook her. It was his holiday home, a place he'd shared with Alison. How insensitive could he get? She didn't stop to think that theirs wasn't a proper marriage. 'You swine, you heartless swine!'

His eyes widened, shocked by her accusation. 'What have I done?'

'How dare you bring me to the same place as your wife? How dare you? I bet you even spent your first honeymoon here.' She rained fists on his chest, her face contorted with anger.

'Nicole.' He caught her hands and stilled their frantic beating. 'Calm down. Stop jumping to conclusions. This is *my* retreat and mine alone. I've never brought anyone here before you.'

'Oh!'

'Is that all you can say?' And still he held her hands against him, and she could feel the strong throb of his heart, and the heat of his body. And, Lord, it felt good.

'I'm sorry.' How pathetic her apology sounded. How pathetic her outburst. She'd overreacted. Why hadn't she ascertained the true facts first? Because as always she'd leapt in without thinking. One day her runaway tongue would get her into serious trouble.

'And so you should be,' he declared sternly. And then he let her hands go. But before she could move away his arms slid around her and held her close to him.

Just that, nothing more, but Nicole's senses surged into overdrive. She knew he was only trying to say, It's all right, it was an understandable mistake, I'm not cross with you; but although her mind knew that her body didn't.

His touch electrified her; it sent her into spasm, it shocked her entire system, and it was a struggle to control herself, to stop herself from snaking her arms around him too and pulling his head down to hers.

She wanted him to kiss her, she wanted to taste him, she wanted to press her body even closer, she wanted to sink into him, she wanted...

Her thoughts trailed uneasily as he abruptly put her from him. Heaven help her, she'd given herself away! And he was quite rightly repulsed by it.

One glance at his face, at the horror stamped on it, at the hardness that glazed his dark eyes, and she knew; she felt mortified, and she didn't know which way to look, which way to turn. In the end she simply ran out of the room, out of the house, down the steps and across the powdery sand.

She stood looking out at the turquoise ocean and wondered how she was going to face him again.

CHAPTER FIVE

Ross was appalled at his own stupidity. What had possessed him to hold Nicole like that? No wonder she'd run, she must be scared witless. So much for his assurance that he wouldn't touch her!

But how could he not want to hold her, kiss her, make love to her, when she was so lovely, so exciting?

Without even realising he was doing it he followed her out of the house, stood a moment on the porch and looked at her standing at the ocean edge. She had kicked off her shoes but she still wore the grey silk suit, and it looked incongruous against such a simple setting.

She should be wearing a sarong, a square of filmy fabric that would cover and invite at the same time, that would torment and tease him, that would mould itself to her body when the soft warm breezes played their magic. Something in blues and greens that would turn her into a sea nymph—*and he was being fanciful.*

Dammit! He couldn't afford to have such feelings. He must never feel anything for Nicole, for anyone. It wasn't safe, it wasn't wise.

Nevertheless he found himself walking towards her, wanting to reassure her. 'Nicole.' He said her name softly. She didn't acknowledge him but he saw the hunch of her shoulders, her sudden stillness, and he knew that she'd heard, that she was still angry.

He took another step, so close now that he could reach out and touch her—and he would have done if he hadn't thought that she would knock his hand furiously away.

'It was a mistake,' he said. 'It won't happen again, I promise.'

And yet how hard he would find it. All these months since Alison's death he'd vowed he would never let himself get close to another woman, and yet after knowing Nicole for only one week he felt a desperate need to bed her.

He hoped and prayed it was no more than that. Lust he could handle. Love he could not.

'I'd prefer you kept away from me,' she informed him coolly.

Ouch! That hurt. But he deserved it. 'A tall order, considering we'll be living in the same house.'

'A deserted one at that,' she flung caustically. 'Good one, Ross. You really thought that out.'

'I wanted you to see it.'

She frowned. 'Why?'

'I thought you'd like it.'

'I do—I would,' she said, 'under different circumstances. But it's hardly a place for non-lovers, is it?' She tossed her head contemptuously. 'A honeymoon in Blackpool would have suited us much better. The lights are on at the moment; every night we could have walked up and down the Golden Mile admiring them and we'd have been perfectly anonymous in the crowds.'

'And we'd have frozen to death. Or drowned in the rain. Isn't this so much nicer?'

'I like Blackpool,' she retorted defensively. 'I like people.'

'This isn't the only house on the island.'

She shrugged. 'Maybe not, but you made damn sure it was well away from the others. If you never brought your wife here who did you bring? Or are you a loner? Do you enjoy the solitude? Do you come here to get away from things?'

'There's so much we don't know about each other,' he said quietly.

Nicole drew in a ragged breath. 'So maybe we ought to sit down right now and get on with it. Let's talk into the night. Let's talk until we know each other's innermost secrets, no skeletons unexposed. And then as soon as it's over we can go home.'

Even as she spoke she marched her way back across the sand to the house.

Ross followed. 'I thought you'd enjoy it here.'

Another toss of her lovely head. 'How can you possibly know what I'd like?'

He'd been afraid something like this might happen. It was the reason he hadn't told her about his plans. He'd known that she would refuse to come, say it wasn't practical, come up with a thousand different excuses.

'I'm generalising. Isn't it the sort of place everyone dreams of?'

She didn't answer; she simply stormed ahead until they were back indoors, and then she sat on one of the cane chairs and glared at him.

He felt sad. He hadn't wanted it to be like this. Her voice had entranced him right from the word go, and she was beginning to get beneath his skin. It was something he found difficult to handle—and he was doing it so damn badly! And he still hadn't found out whether she had anything on underneath her silk jacket!

'I think maybe we ought to unpack and get into something more comfortable,' he suggested.

'I'm not planning on staying.'

Brows rose tellingly. 'I'm afraid you have no choice. There's no other plane out today. In fact there's only one a week.'

Nicole jumped to her feet in high dudgeon, eyes blazing.

'I can't believe this. I can't believe you're doing this to me.'

'I'm not doing anything, Nicole,' he said quietly. 'You're doing it to yourself.'

She glared at him for a defiant second, and then seemed to deflate. Slowly she headed for the bedroom, closing the door resolutely behind her. A second later it opened again. 'Don't even begin to think about coming in,' she warned.

'No damn lock on the door,' Nicole muttered as she un-snapped locks and unzipped her case. 'No privacy.' Case flung open. 'One bedroom.' Undies thrown into a drawer. *Undies he had packed!* 'One bed.' Tops and skirts rammed on to hangers. *Clothes he'd picked out of her wardrobe for her! And some she'd never seen before!* 'What sort of game is he playing?' Toiletries slammed down in the bathroom—the only bathroom! No lock here either?

She was furious—with both him and herself. Herself for responding to him so wantonly, and Ross for putting her in this situation. Talk, he'd said. For heaven's sake, they couldn't talk for a whole week. What would they find to say? She could relate her life story in five minutes.

'Are you finished?' His voice came from the other side of the door, and she thought she saw the handle move.

'No, I haven't,' she yelled.

'I've made you a drink.'

Was she being unreasonable?

'It's nicely chilled.'

Meaning she needed to cool down?

'I'll be out in a minute.' But first a shower and a change of clothes.

In less than five minutes she rejoined him, the silk suit replaced by a blue cotton sundress which echoed the colour of her eyes, her still wet hair clinging to her shapely head, her face devoid of make-up.

She gave him a faint, wary smile. 'That's better,' she said. 'I was so hot and bothered.' She'd decided that getting angry was no answer to her problem. A cool friendliness was in order. Nothing that would encourage him to touch or kiss, but nothing to get his back up either. Surely she could manage that?

She sat down and picked up the drink Ross had made for her. It was long and cool and refreshing and she drank half of it in one go. He watched her every movement. In fact his eyes hadn't left her since she'd returned, scrutinising, appraising, playing havoc with her senses. 'The bathroom's yours if you want to use it,' she said calmly. And felt proud that she'd managed to hide her concern.

'I might do that.' He hauled himself lazily to his feet, took his empty glass to the kitchen, and then crossed in front of her to the bedroom.

Nicole wished the bathroom was separate. It could be tricky if she was in bed when he wanted to use it. She didn't even consider the fact that he would share the bed with her. That was a non-starter from the word go.

She took her drink out on to the veranda, sat on a canvas chair and looked out at the almost still ocean, with its shimmering blues and greens, and compared it to the crashing grey waters of the Atlantic they'd left behind.

She looked at the cloudless cerulean sky—seen only once in a blue moon in England. This last summer had been dreadful. Grey skies and rain and only a few sunny days.

And she looked at the glorious white sand stretching away on either side with its two sets of footprints. At St Meek there was sand, yes, but much coarser, much darker, and also the remains of a sea wall, derelict fishing boats, seaweed-covered rocks, and shallow pools left behind by the outgoing tide which Aaron investigated to his heart's content.

And she knew which she liked best.

'What are you thinking?'

He had come up silently behind her and given Nicole a start. Would he believe her if she said that she'd been thinking of home, that she preferred Cornwall, even in the height of summer with all the noisy holidaymakers, to this secluded tropical island?

She doubted it. This was his private paradise and he wouldn't take kindly to anyone putting it down. So instead of answering his question she said, 'What made you buy this place?'

He'd brought two more drinks out, and he placed them on the wide wooden rail that fenced the veranda and then dropped into a chair. 'I needed an escape.'

'From what?' The moment she asked the question Nicole knew it was a mistake.

A bleak shadow darkened his face and he seemed to sag and sink even more deeply into his seat. 'From my sins.'

This wasn't quite what she'd expected. 'Your sins?'

A moment's hesitation, then, 'I killed my wife and daughter.'

Nicole instantly turned to look at him, to express disbelief, but when she saw his tortured expression she knew better than to say anything. If he wanted to explain himself he would, in his own time. So she sat silent and waited.

It was a long silence.

'I was driving,' he said finally, 'when the accident happened.' He'd changed into denim shorts and a T-shirt, but Nicole hardly noticed, saw only the horror in his eyes.

'You cannot blame yourself for that,' she said at once. 'There are hundreds of road traffic accidents every day. People—'

'Oh, but I can and I do,' he cut in vehemently. 'A lorry pulled out in front of us. I slammed on the brakes, but not quickly enough. I'd been drinking, you see. My reflexes were impaired.'

Nicole was stunned. 'You were guilty of drunk driving?' She hadn't known that.

'No, dammit, of course I wasn't. I wasn't even over the limit. But I'd had a glass of wine over lunch.'

'And you think that if you hadn't it would have made a difference?'

'Yes. No. I don't know. I know I blame myself. I always will. Nothing will change that.'

'I think you're wrong,' said Nicole quietly. 'And I think that if your wife knew how you were torturing yourself she'd say the same.'

He shrugged. 'I cannot help it.'

'Perhaps you dwell on the accident too much?'

'Wouldn't you?'

Nicole grimaced. 'I don't know. I hope you don't let Aaron see how much you're hurting. It's not good for kids to be subjected to—'

'Of course I don't,' he interjected swiftly, angrily. 'But the whole idea of this honeymoon—holiday—is so that I can explain. So that when I have black moods you'll know why, or when I yell at you for no particular reason then you'll hopefully understand. It's essential that you know this.'

'I can see the logic,' said Nicole, 'but you didn't have to bring me here to tell me.'

'I did. Here is the only place where there are no memories of Alison and Tara. Here I can be myself. Here, hopefully, you will get to know the true me.'

Nicole wasn't sure what he meant, or even whether she liked the sound of it, but for the moment she said nothing. He seemed to be living in some sort of hell, and if she could help him drive out his demons then at least she would have achieved something.

'So you bought this place after the accident?'

He nodded. 'I spent three months here. But then Tilda became ill and I was forced to return.'

'Would you have gone back to England otherwise?'

'Eventually, when I'd come to terms with things.'

'Poor Aaron.'

Ross frowned. 'What do you mean?'

'He lost his mother, his grandmother, and must have thought he'd lost you.'

'He had Tilda,' came the defensive answer. 'And I regularly spoke to him on the telephone. Which reminds me—I must phone Tilda, let her know we've arrived safely, see how they both are.'

'It still must have been painful for him.' insisted Nicole. 'It's good to see he dotes on you now.'

'He's a good kid.'

'You spoil him. I've never seen a child with so many toys. They don't compensate for love, Ross.'

'I know that,' he retorted defensively. 'I'll go and make that call. I'll have to go into town. Is there anything you need?'

'There's no phone here?'

'No,' he answered shortly. 'And that's the way I like it.'

Maybe when he'd bought the house it had been what he wanted, but now, with Tilda ill, surely it would be expedient to have a phone installed? Or how about his mobile? Wouldn't that work here?

'I didn't bring it,' he said, as if reading her thoughts. 'Do you want anything or not?'

'I think I'd like to come with you,' said Nicole. It would give her an opportunity to see more of the island.

'Another time,' he told her crisply, and the next moment he had gone.

It had upset him, talking about his dead wife, thought Nicole. He needed time to himself; she ought to have realised that. She would make a point of being extra nice to him when he returned.

She would prepare a meal. Perhaps a barbecue on the beach would be nice. Less intimate, more fun, and the fresh air would make them tired and they'd fall asleep the instant they went to bed. Hopefully.

Exploring the fridge, Nicole found plenty of salad ingredients, as well as what looked like a red snapper, which would be perfect grilled, and there was fresh bread, lots of fruit, just about everything they would need.

When Ross returned she was busy mixing a salad dressing. 'How's Tilda?' she asked cheerfully over her shoulder.

'Good. Except that I think I woke her up. I'd forgotten the time difference.'

'And Aaron?'

'Not even missing us. The woman from the agency arrived and Aaron and her son disappeared into his room and weren't seen again. He'll be no trouble. Oh, and your friends sent a message saying they hope the story works out well, whatever that means?'

Nicole felt her cheeks colour and was thankful she had her back to him. The last thing Ross needed was to believe she'd married him for any other reason than to help him out in his time of need.'

'What did they mean? What story?'

It was obvious he wasn't going to let this pass. Nicole had to think quickly. 'I—I, er, told them I was making up a story for Aaron.'

'I didn't know you could write?'

She shrugged. 'It probably won't be any good.' She quickly changed the subject. 'I thought we'd barbecue our supper. I've been getting things ready. Would you mind setting up the barbecue?'

The evening passed pleasantly. Ross's black mood had gone and he was good company. They took a swim in the

ocean before their meal and then ate sitting cross-legged
on the sand.

They watched the sun streak the sea with gold and red
and purple before it finally dipped below the horizon, and
then it was the sky's turn to change to a myriad different
colours. It was quite spectacular, and it would have been
even better had Ross's arm been about her, her head resting
on his shoulder. It was a spell-binding magical moment,
and one that should have been shared.

It was dark by the time they went indoors and Nicole's
nerves began to skitter. Bedtime was approaching and she
was worried. This was, to all intents and purposes, their
wedding night. But as this was no ordinary wedding sleeping together was not part of the plan. What else were they
to do, though, when there was only one bed?

'Have you ever slept beneath the stars, Nicole?'

She looked at him, startled. 'When I was a kid we went
camping. Does that count?'

'Nope. I mean as a grown-up?'

'Then my answer's no. What are you suggesting? That
we sleep out here tonight?' It was certainly warm enough.

'That *I* sleep out here. It won't be the first time. I have
a hammock I usually sling on the veranda. It's amazingly
comfortable, so long as I don't thrash around too much,
otherwise I end up on the deck,' he added wryly.

'You don't have to,' she said quietly. 'Let me take the
hammock.'

'I wouldn't dream of it.'

'It's your bed.'

'And it will be my pleasure letting you sleep in it, Mrs
Dufrais.'

If he hadn't tagged on *Mrs Dufrais* she wouldn't have
said any more, but she felt he was pointing out how awkward she was being. 'I suppose we could share it,' she said

dubiously, her heart beating double quick time at the thought.

'Tempting.' His lips curved and he looked as though he much preferred her suggestion to his.

Nicole felt her blood run first hot and then cold, her stomach muscles contracting as imagination took over. What was she letting herself in for?

'But I make it a rule never to fraternise with my employees. The bed is yours; the hammock's mine. No arguments.' The smile had gone, his face turning cold and impassive.

Relief flooded and anger burgeoned both at the same time. She hated being reminded that he was employing her, that she was a wife in name only and it meant not a thing to him. 'That suits me just fine.' Her tone was as clipped as his. 'In fact I might go to bed now. I'll just clear these things away and then—'

'I'll do them.'

'No, it's all right, I—'

'Nicole!'

She shrugged. 'Whatever you wish. Goodnight, Ross.'

'Goodnight, wife.'

Nicole was in bed when the door quietly opened and Ross crept in. She sat bolt upright. Although she'd switched off the lamp an almost full moon shone like daylight and she could see him clearly. 'What do you think you're doing?'

Ross stopped and looked towards the bed. 'I'm sorry, did I disturb you? I tried to be quiet.'

'You shouldn't be here.'

'I needed the bathroom.'

'Oh.' She felt slightly foolish.

'May I be permitted to use it?' he asked with a wry grin.

'Stop it. You don't have to ask. I'm sorry.'

He came towards her. 'Couldn't you sleep?' His voice was oddly concerned.

Nicole shook her head. 'Strange bed and all that.'

'And so much has happened today.' He sat down on the edge.

Nicole froze.

'Are you regretting it already?'

'No.' She wished he would go.

'You're very tense.'

'Is it surprising?'

'You know I wish you no harm.'

'Would you mind just using the bathroom and getting out?'

'Afraid of me, Nicole?' There was the faintest smile in his voice.

Afraid of herself more likely. This enforced togetherness was playing havoc with her senses. Beneath the sheets she was trembling and she was scared he might notice. She wasn't falling in love with him or anything like that, but, Lord, she wanted him.

And it didn't please her. She wasn't the type to hop easily into bed with every man she met, not like some girls she knew. She had to be in love to allow a man the freedom of her body. There'd only ever been two, and in each instance they'd been the ones to end the relationship. She'd been broken-hearted on each occasion, only afterwards realising that it was all for the best, that she had never truly loved them, not the sort of love that lasted a lifetime. The sort Ross had felt for Alison!

Would he ever fall in love again? Somehow she doubted it, and it made her position here all the sadder.

'Why should I be afraid of you?' she asked.

'No reason. None at all. But it's an impression I get.'

She forced a smile. 'An entirely erroneous one.'

'If you're sure.' He pushed himself up but he continued to look at her and Nicole knew that he didn't believe a word she'd said. Then to her consternation he lowered his head to hers. Panic set in, and she was preparing to fight him off when his lips touched her forehead in the lightest of kisses. 'Goodnight, Nicole. I shan't disturb you again. Pleasant dreams.'

He crossed to the bathroom and a few minutes later he came out again; without even looking towards the bed he disappeared.

Contrarily, Nicole felt disappointed.

Lord, that had been hard. How he'd walked away from Nicole, Ross didn't know. She was right; it had been a bad idea coming away on honeymoon.

His main aim, without a doubt, had been to please his aunt, and he'd thought that while they were here it would provide the perfect opportunity to discover more about each other: hidden depths, likes, dislikes, everything there was to know. He'd not expected to find himself so damned attracted to her that all he wanted to do was jump into her bed, to act rather than talk!

During the last twelve months he'd not felt remotely like making love to any woman, even though there'd been several who'd given the hint that they were interested. So why did Nicole affect him like this? Perhaps because she'd shown complete uninterest? Could that be it? Was he intrigued? Did he want to find out what it would take to light her fires? But what if in the process he fell in love with her?

He knew that he should get on with his life but he was too afraid—afraid that it would happen again, that he would lose again, and that the next time it would destroy him altogether. Much better to keep her at arm's length.

Halfway through the night he was woken by a sound. He didn't know what, and he lay there listening in case it happened again. But all he could hear was the gentle whoosh of the ocean. And then he saw her. Nicole walking towards him—stark naked. And when she reached the hammock she began to climb into it.

CHAPTER SIX

NICOLE was mortified. She hadn't sleepwalked in years, not since she was a child. It had begun when she was being bullied at school, but gradually over the years she'd done it less and less often, until she couldn't remember the last time it had happened.

So why now? And to attempt to get into bed with Ross! With nothing on! Hot colour swept her cheeks at the very thought. Although, to give him his due, he'd been a perfect gentleman, ignoring her state of undress, walking her back to the bedroom, talking gently, encouragingly, and then sitting with her until she fell asleep again.

Thank goodness he'd realised what was happening. She smiled now at the thought of attempting to make love in a hammock. They'd probably have both ended up on the deck!

It's not funny, she told herself sternly. It was something to worry about, not laugh at. *And what if it happened again? What if he wasn't so considerate the next time?* It must have been hard for him to ignore her nudity. He could quite easily have taken advantage. The thought was enough to send a chill down her spine.

The morning sun was already high in the sky, and the huge fan above her bed stirred the air and made it minimally less humid. *The fan!* She'd switched it off last night because the noise had kept her awake. And she was quite sure Ross hadn't put it on when he'd walked her back to bed. Which meant only one thing. He'd been in here again while she slept.

It was going to happen, she knew, because of the bathroom, but the thought that he'd entered, possibly even stood looking down at her, sent her into further turmoil. She fervently hoped that seeing her naked last night hadn't given him any ideas.

Uneasy now, she rolled out of bed and padded across the bare boards to the bathroom. She showered, brushed her teeth, towel-dried her hair, then came to a full-stop when she returned to the bedroom and found Ross standing there.

Her eyes blazed in defence even though her heart slipped into top gear. 'What are you doing here?' She could have added *again*, but she didn't.

'I need to use the bathroom.'

'So you thought you'd queue up?' she asked testily, not liking the way he was looking at her, as though he was seeing the woman beneath the loosely knotted towel, the woman he had seen last night in all her naked glory.

'Let me assure you, Ross Dufrais,' she further fumed, 'this isn't a waiting room. If you want this room, then you can have it. *I'll* sleep on the hammock in future.'

'Except that your clothes would still be here, and you'd need the bathroom. Positions reversed.' He didn't look in the least put out; in fact he looked distinctly amused. 'I think it's a case of making the best of the situation.'

'And "the best" includes invading my privacy? Couldn't you have waited?' Her blue eyes flashed furiously. As far as she was concerned there was nothing remotely funny in the situation.

'I was lying when I said I needed the bathroom,' he confessed. 'I actually came in to find a shirt.'

But he'd lingered long enough to catch her half naked!

'I'm going now,' he added unconcernedly. 'Breakfast will be ready in five minutes.'

He slipped out before she could say more, and it was a distinctly disgruntled Nicole who pulled a lilac and purple shift over her head. She wasn't sure that she understood

Ross. Yesterday he'd almost sunk into depression, and yet this morning he was teasing her. And she didn't want to be teased; she didn't feel like being teased. She was cross because he... Her thoughts skidded to a halt. Because he what? *Because he disturbed her?*

The answer had to be yes.

She'd gone to sleep thinking about him, imagining what it would be like to be made love to by him, she'd even dreamt about him doing it—and that was something else, because it had been fantastic. Then, horror of horrors, she'd gone to him in her sleep. That part didn't bear thinking about. And she certainly wasn't looking forward to eating breakfast with him. The whole situation was fast becoming an embarrassment.

But she needn't have worried. Ross didn't mention the previous night; he said nothing to make her feel uncomfortable. In fact he did everything he could to put her at her ease. And for the next few days things remained that way. Much to her chagrin!

They swam, they explored, they talked at length. There was one heart-stopping moment when he asked her what she'd done for a living before she'd walked out on her lascivious boss. But she managed to brush it off lightly by saying, 'Just an office job. Nothing very interesting. I really don't want to talk about it.'

And he accepted that. They laughed a lot, and, more importantly, they became friends. But nothing more. Contrarily Nicole wanted more. Her physical need of him increased daily, hourly almost, and more than once she caught him looking at her with the same sort of hunger. It was always instantly wiped off his face, but she knew that she wasn't mistaken.

On the last day he took her sailing in a borrowed boat, and although what happened was an accident Nicole thought afterwards that she couldn't have orchestrated it any better if she'd tried.

Looking at Ross instead of where she was going, Nicole tripped over a coiled rope and fell—straight into his arms.

He groaned, mumbled something about fate, and then crushed her against him.

The instant he did so every one of Nicole's senses went into red alert. Dangerous! Taboo! Fateful! But she did nothing about it. She'd been going crazy all week imagining being made love to by him. She'd lain in bed at night fantasising. And now that he was actually holding her she wasn't going to spoil the moment.

'Nicole!' He muttered her name thickly as his mouth sought hers. Contact was dynamite. It felt as though he'd lit a whole display of fireworks. She felt herself exploding from within. A deep, uncontrollable heat started in the very core of her and spread until it reached every extremity.

She drank thirstily, greedily from his mouth, feeling as though nothing would satisfy her. She'd waited too long; emotions long held in check now spiralled out of control.

'Nicole?' It was an urgent, throbbing question as he dragged his mouth from hers.

He was having second thoughts! But she couldn't stop now, didn't want to stop, *wouldn't*! 'Yes, Ross. *Yes!*' she breathed. And this time *she* claimed *his* mouth and the fireworks began all over again.

The heat that sizzled through her was like nothing she'd ever experienced. White-hot and petrifying, boiling her blood, searing her skin, sending her spinning into outer space.

As their lips and tongues melded his hands urgently explored, tracing the shape of her face, her straining throat with its frenetic pulse, the soft swell of her thrusting, aching breasts, her hips, her bottom.

She in turn ran her fingers through the coarse wiriness

of his hair, over tightly muscled shoulders, down the length
of his solid back, feeling, wanting, needing.

Her heart beat so loudly it hurt; every pulse made itself
felt. She was a throbbing mass of sensation so intense that
it scared her. And yet still she did not want to pull away.

Hunger this deep had never filled her before. It was as
though every dream, every fantasy, every thought, even,
that she'd had about Ross during the past couple of weeks
had culminated in this deep, soul-defying need. And there
was nothing she could do to stop herself.

What made it even more magical was that Ross's thirst
was as great as her own. His mouth bruised and demanded
and took. She could feel him trembling, feel the powerful
beat of his heart slamming against his ribcage, the heat of
him, the wickedly exciting surge of his manhood.

One hand still held her close while his other urgently
sought the swell of her breast. All she wore was a thin T-
shirt, but he cursed softly at the hindrance and with a swift
economical tug the shirt flew over her head and was flung
to goodness knew where. Her skimpy bra followed, and
then with a sigh of satisfaction he let his hand stake its
claim.

Fresh shudders of pleasure ripped through Nicole's veins
like hot molten metal as he stroked his thumb in erotic
circles over her sensitised nipples, as his mouth sought hers
once again.

It was more than she could cope with. She didn't know
which she enjoyed the most, his kisses or what he was
doing to her breasts. With a cry she wrested her mouth from
his and flung her head back.

Immediately Ross traced his tongue and lips down the
arched column of her quivering throat, seared a line between her aching breasts, and finally sucked one throbbing
nipple into his mouth, where he proceeded to nibble and
bite and send her mindless with pleasure.

Nicole cried out again and again. She clutched his head and whimpered like a baby. She bowed down and kissed his hair—and then suddenly they were both thrown off balance.

Her eyes snapped open and she clung to Ross for support. He managed to grip the rail and keep them upright. The boat had grounded. It had come to a crunching halt on the sandy beach. Their sudden journey to heaven had made them both forget where they were and what they should be doing.

'Get dressed,' he rasped, and it was as though the past few minutes had never happened. The desire had gone from his dark velvet eyes and he was looking at her as though she had no right to be semi-clad.

Nicole clenched her teeth and turned around to look for her shirt and bra, only to discover them floating in the ocean about fifty yards out. She was damned if she was going to swim after them. Ross had ripped them off, he could fetch them—or put up with her as she was.

'What are you playing at?' The harshness was still in his voice.

Nicole glared. 'Nothing. I love standing around like this.' She felt like crossing her arms over her breasts, but she didn't. What was the point when he'd explored every inch? She stood tall and proud instead, and continued to glare, almost daring him to drop his eyes and look at her.

Naturally he didn't. 'Dammit, Nicole, this is no time for games.'

'I'm not playing, Ross. My clothes are out there, where you flung them.'

His eyes followed her pointing finger and he looked momentarily shocked at what he'd done, but no apologies were made. 'You'd best get back to the house,' he said roughly instead.

'Why? Don't you need help?' Nicole found surprising

pleasure in taunting him, knowing the conflicting emotions that were warring within him. It gave her an odd feeling of power.

'I can manage.'

She sidled up to him. 'If you're quite sure?'

'I'm sure,' he grated, keeping his eyes strictly on hers, making no attempt to look at where his mouth had been earlier.

Nicole could almost feel the effort it took him and she smiled as she turned away, secure now in the knowledge that he found her attractive. If nothing else it proved he was finally beginning to get over his wife's death. And that had to be a good thing.

It had been a foolish mistake, a very foolish one. All week he'd managed to keep control. He didn't want to become involved with Nicole, he couldn't afford to—and yet she was so damned attractive that there were times when she drove him insane.

This honeymoon had been a bad idea. It would have been far better to suffer Tilda's remonstrations than this. How he'd thought he would get away with a whole week in Nicole's presence when he was already beginning to find her irresistible he didn't know.

And now this! He shovelled like a maniac, trying to free the boat. What an idiot he was. What had possessed him? What had made him do it? He'd virtually fallen on her. He'd kissed her like a starving man in the desert who'd suddenly found food. He'd stripped her, for heaven's sake! How was he ever going to face her again?

With a bit more shoving and pushing and digging, and a lot of cursing, the boat rode free. He climbed aboard and took it a little further along the coast to the neighbour from whom he'd borrowed it.

And then, with shoulders firmed, he marched back to the

house. He was not looking forward to this. He had lots of apologies to make, assurances to give. The odd thing about it was that Nicole hadn't pushed him away; she'd been as eager as he to kiss and touch and taste. It was probably the romance of the island that had done it to her. Once they were home they would each be glad of some distance between them.

As he mounted the steps Nicole was on the veranda waiting. She looked enchanting in a soft green filmy dress, and despite all his good intentions a flurry of desire packed Ross's stomach.

'Nicole.' He was firm in his resolve. 'I want to apologise again for what happened. It was unforgivable.'

'It was,' she agreed with a small smile, 'but also rather wonderful. I don't know why you're apologising.' And she walked towards him as though she wanted him to kiss her again.

His stomach lurched. He didn't want to turn down such an open invitation but knew that he must. He held up a hand, and with his tone carefully neutral said, 'I mean it, Nicole. It was a mistake, a big mistake. It won't happen again.' But how he wished that it could. How he wished that he could lose himself in her, find—

'You're being hard on yourself.'

Her swift appraisal of the situation surprised him. 'Maybe,' he admitted with a shrug, 'but I still mean what I said. I don't intend entering into an affair with you—which is all it would be.'

'An affair?' Her finely shaped brows rose; her lovely eyes widened. 'You're my husband.'

He winced. He was being unfair on her. But she'd known the rules before she became involved. 'In name only, Nicole,' he said quietly, determinedly. 'Don't ever forget that.'

'As if you'd let me,' she muttered, in a voice so soft he

was sure she hadn't intended him to hear, and with that she swung away and went inside the house.

He followed more slowly, and was careful to keep his distance for the rest of the evening. Tomorrow they were flying back to England. Tomorrow his torment would be over.

Wishful thinking on his part. When they arrived home and he took their cases upstairs he discovered that in their absence Tilda had had his bedroom redecorated and purchased a new double bed. She'd moved in Nicole's clothes and everything else belonging to her. There were flowers in a vase and it all looked fresh and inviting and hopelessly romantic. It filled him with dread. He'd been kind of hoping they would carry on with their separate rooms.

He said nothing to Nicole; she was busy playing with Aaron and telling Matilda all about their honeymoon, emphasising what a good time they'd had. He was grateful to her for keeping up the pretence. But they were both tired, and as soon as Aaron had been put to bed Nicole announced she was going too.

What did he do now? Wait and let her discover their sleeping arrangements for herself? Or accompany her and apologise for his aunt's interference?

In the end he had no choice. Matilda kept him talking, and although he wanted to scold her when she asked whether he liked the room he hadn't the heart. 'It was quite a surprise,' he said instead.

'Do you think Nicole will approve?' Tilda sounded worried.

'I'm sure she will.'

'I think you should go and join her.'

'And how about you?' The last thing he wanted was to share a bed with Nicole—sexy, exciting Nicole. It would be best if he waited until she was asleep. 'Isn't it time you went to bed?'

Matilda nodded. 'Just help me upstairs and I'll manage.'

And so he helped his aunt, but he went back down again, and it was a couple of hours later before he finally climbed the stairs and forced himself to enter the bedroom which had once been his private domain but now held the woman he'd married. The woman who was gradually stealing his heart. And no matter how good it felt it was something he couldn't allow to happen.

Nicole had unthinkingly gone to the room she'd slept in before their wedding and had been both surprised and amused to discover that her belongings had been removed. And when she ventured into Ross's room and saw the double bed she almost laughed out aloud. Good old Aunt Matilda!

Ross had vowed never to touch her again. Would that be possible if they slept in the same bed? And how would she feel about it? She was in grave danger of falling in love with Ross. Sleeping together could very well be the catalyst.

Did she want to love a man who would never love her? Could she walk away from him with her heart in one piece when her contract finished? The answer to both questions had to be no. But what could she do about it?

Slowly she undressed and climbed into bed, lying on the very edge so that Ross would have plenty of room. Her heart was unsteady and she lay awake for ages, wondering what he would do. But gradually her eyes closed and sleep took over.

What it was that woke her Nicole wasn't sure. She looked at the clock. It was after two, and Ross hadn't yet come to bed. But there was the noise again. She sat up. And in the faint light of the moon she could just make out Ross asleep in the armchair tucked into one of the room's alcoves. He looked extremely uncomfortable, one leg dan-

gling over an arm, the other stretched out in front, his head
hanging at an awkward angle. He grunted as he shifted
position.

Nicole couldn't let him sleep like that. 'Ross.'

No answer.

She slipped out of bed and touched his arm. 'Ross.'

'Mmm?'

'Wake up, Ross.'

He was suddenly alert and ready to jump up. 'Is it Aaron
or Tilda?'

'Neither,' she assured him quietly. 'But you can't sleep
there; you'll ache like an old man in the morning. Come
to bed.'

'You know what will happen if I do?'

Nicole shook her head firmly. 'No, it won't.' But, yes,
she wanted it to. 'We'll put the pillows between us, if you
like, but you can't sleep here; that's a fact. I won't let you.'

He growled something unintelligible but then hauled
himself up. 'If you're quite sure.' And she thought he
looked relieved.

'I am sure.'

But once he was beside her, even though he lay carefully
on his side and she on hers, Nicole began to have her
doubts. They weren't even touching and yet she could feel
him. Feel his presence, feel the exciting sexiness of him.
How could she sleep under those circumstances?

But sleep she did. The long day travelling had taken its
toll and her eyelids drooped and she knew no more. It was
light when she next opened her eyes—and there was something heavy over her body.

She realised, as she lay there in shocked stillness, that
they were both facing the same way: her back against
Ross's chest, his knees behind hers, his arm across her—
with his hand on her breast!

How did she get out of that without waking him? He

would be full of abject apologies if he knew, that went
without saying. But somehow in his sleep he had turned
and held her and now she was afraid to move.

So she lay still and pretended to be asleep. Not the eas-
iest of things when a man who could arouse her with a
single touch was holding her breast. Not only holding, but
stroking, caressing, feeding her hunger. And it became
gradually apparent that he was aroused too. Very much so.
And it suddenly dawned on her that he wasn't asleep—he
was awake! And he was naked!

What now? Ought she to let him know that she was
awake too? Ought she to go along with it? Or ought she to
scramble out of bed as quick as she could?

'Are you awake, Nicole?' His voice, soft as a summer
breeze, sounded close to her ear.

She waited a long moment before answering huskily,
'Yes.'

'I want to say I'm sorry for—for touching you like this,
but I can't.'

There was a pause and then, when she made no response,
'Hell, Nicole, I find you irresistible, and I want to make
love to you. But I cannot promise you love. You do know
that?' His fingers continued to torment.

Another husky whisper. Another 'Yes.'

'So if you want me to stop just say the word.'

Nicole knew that the safest, wisest course would be to
move away from him, avoid this situation in future. But
sanity didn't enter into it. She accepted what Ross was
saying about never falling in love again, but she wasn't in
love with him either. Attracted, yes, but not in love. So
why couldn't they enjoy their marriage as it should be enjoyed and then walk away at the end of it?

Don't be stupid, said an inner voice. *How is that possible? You* are *in love with him.* No, I'm not, she retorted.

Yes, you are.

But she wasn't; she knew she wasn't. She'd only known him two weeks, for heaven's sake! It was nothing more than chemical attraction. Pretty potent, but definitely nothing more. So why shouldn't she allow him to make love to her? Why make a hardship of their marriage when it wasn't necessary? Why not take what was offered and enjoy it?

'I don't want you to stop.' The words came out on an agonised breath.

And as though he'd been holding his own breath, waiting for her answer, Ross exhaled deeply and his arm about her tightened. 'You're very sure, Nicole?'

'I'm sure.'

And then his lips nuzzled the back of her neck, and her ears, and he turned her to face him and their mouths came together and she tasted the maleness of this man who was beginning to mean so much to her. *No! He didn't, he mustn't. It wasn't part of the agreement.* The thought came and went with equal quickness.

His hands explored, tracing with ever-mounting urgency the soft feminine shape of her, her face, her throat, her thrusting, aching breasts. Her satin nightie was barely a restriction, but impatiently it was removed.

By now the quilt was tossed away and the cool air met her burning skin and added to the torment building inside her. She shivered with sheer pleasure and her hands clawed at Ross, raked through his thick hair, her arms wrapping around him, claiming him, letting him know that she was as hungry for love as he was. She moved against him, unconsciously erotic, hearing him gasp, discovering a never before felt desperate need. His hair-roughened chest against the softness of her breasts, against her sensitised nipples, was the most exquisite torture. They had never throbbed so painfully, begged to be touched so frenziedly, screamed so urgently to be sucked into his mouth, to—

'Oh, Nicole,' he groaned, 'what are you doing to me?'

Not as much as he was doing to her. That wasn't possible. This touching of bodies went beyond the realms of imagination. She'd thought about him making love to her, she'd fantasised about it, but nothing had prepared her for the reality. And he hadn't even started!

Their mouths fed feverishly off each other. She felt the growing urgency of him against her thighs—and in the distance she thought she heard Aaron call out. But it might have been herself. Perhaps it was. She didn't hear it again, and Ross gave no indication that he'd heard anything.

He was creating a trail of destruction as his mouth left hers to make its insidious way to her breasts. And then the sucking began, and the nibbling, and the torment and the torture.

Her whole body trembled and became racked with pain which wasn't pain, which was sheer, unadulterated pleasure—and yet it hurt, and she wanted it to go on hurting. It was like a miniature explosion taking place, and shock wave after shock wave moved through her with ever-increasing pressure.

When he had drunk his fill of her breasts his mouth moved slowly down her body, grazing, licking, tasting, pausing at the hollow of her navel, and then on again to the dark triangle of curls that kept secret the pulsing heart of her. Her secret. Soon to be his.

An exploratory finger parted the curls, found the hot moistness waiting for him, delved, played, teased, tormented, sent her into a frenzy of need and desire. She was no longer touching him. She lay back and enjoyed, her legs parted, her lips parted, her breathing shallow and rapid. 'Oh, God, Ross! Oh, God!'

'Am I hurting you?' He stopped for a moment to look at her, his eyes glazed with desire and yet oddly clearer than she'd ever seen them.

'No, no. Go on. Please, go on.'

He needed no more bidding. But this time it was his tongue that entered her, that sent her wild, that threatened to send her out of her mind. Her body thrashed as fresh waves of intense sensation ripped through every part of her.

And then he withdrew and the feelings began to subside. Until he slid his body over her and entered her and the pulsing ecstasy started all over again.

It was only seconds before Ross joined her in cataclysmic sensation, before he too became filled with shock waves and collapsed on top of her.

The aftermath lasted a long time, it seemed like for ever, but eventually Ross slid off her and lay at her side with his hands bunched into fists and buried against his eyes.

He regretted it!

It wouldn't happen again.

It had been a moment of madness as far as he was concerned.

'Ross.' She touched him gently, stroked a finger over his still sweat-slicked shoulder. 'It's all right.'

'No, it's not all right, dammit. I shouldn't have done that. Or at least I should have taken precautions. Dammit, Nicole, why didn't you stop me?'

'Because I wanted you to make to love to me,' she said.

'Why?'

'Why?' she echoed. 'Surely that's obvious? It's the same reason you wanted to make love to me. I think it's called attraction. It's a biological thing, a chemical reaction. You don't have to be in love to want to make love.'

'But—you and me—it shouldn't have—I promised—you trusted me—you—'

Nicole placed a finger over his lips. 'Ross, shh. I've no complaints.' Except maybe a teeny hint of unease that they hadn't used any protection. But she wouldn't tell him that.

He sat up abruptly and stared straight ahead. 'It won't happen again.'

'That would be a shame.'

His head jerked in her direction. 'What are you saying?'

'That I want you to make love to me again—frequently. We'll be careful, we won't make any unwanted babies, but I don't see why we shouldn't *pretend* to have a normal marriage.'

Her emphasis on the word 'pretend' brought a wry smile to his lips. 'If you're sure, Nicole? The last thing I want to do is hurt you.'

'You'd hurt me if you ignored me,' she said quietly.

'An impossible feat, sharing the same bed,' he growled. 'You're a witch, do you know that? I had such high principles when I climbed in beside you, but the intoxicating womanly smell of you, the provocative warmth of you, the heavenly touch of you—they were all my undoing.'

Nicole nodded. 'That's as it should be.'

'Why, you—' He grabbed her then, and his kiss silenced whatever he'd been going to say.

But this time Nicole definitely heard Aaron calling for his grandfather. Ross heard too, and it was with reluctance that they parted, pulled on their robes, and went looking for him.

They found him in Tilda's room, sitting on her bed playing with one of his cars.

Tilda smiled at them knowingly. 'I had to restrain this little monster from coming in to you earlier. Did you sleep well?' It was clear from her expression that she knew exactly what they'd been up to.

Had they made a noise? wondered Nicole as swift colour flooded her cheeks. Or did their lovemaking shine from their eyes?

Ross, on the other hand, looked not in the least concerned. 'We slept wonderfully well, thank you. And as for you, you little rascal, what are you doing up so early?'

'Early?' questioned Matilda with a lift of her thin brows. 'It's nine-fifteen. Long past little boys' breakfast time.'

CHAPTER SEVEN

'EXCUSE me, miss, is this yours?'

Nicole whirled around and a man whom she'd previously seen watching them was holding out her camera. She frowned, because she hadn't realised that it was missing.

'It was on those rocks—and I saw you taking pictures of your son earlier. I guessed it must be yours.'

'He's not my son.' The words were out before she could stop them.

'I'm sorry, a natural mistake. But in any case you wouldn't want to lose your camera. Pictures of kids are very precious.'

'Thank you, you're most kind.' The man was in his midtwenties, about the same height as Ross, with dark blond hair and a pleasant face, and he looked curiously now at Aaron as he came running to her side.

He smiled at the boy, who had taken Nicole's hand before looking up at the stranger.

'This man found my camera, Aaron. Silly me. I left it over there.'

'Aaron?' said the man. 'That's a fine name.'

'Aaron Dufrais,' announced Aaron, with an unconscious proud tilt of his head that reminded Nicole of Ross.

Looking down at her small charge with a fond smile, she missed the man's sudden frown.

'How old are you, Aaron Dufrais?'

'Three. How old are you?'

The man laughed. 'He's not backward at coming forward, is he? His parents must be very proud of him.'

Nicole had no intention of discussing anything so personal with a stranger. She glanced at her watch. 'I must get him home,' she said. 'Thanks again for returning my camera. Come along, Aaron.'

'Bye-bye, Aaron,' said the man. 'Here.' And he tossed him a coin. 'Buy yourself some sweets.'

It was a pound, too much to give such a young child, especially someone he didn't know. Nicole wanted to take it from Aaron and hand it back, but the boy's eyes were wide and so pleased that she hadn't the heart. 'You shouldn't have done that,' she said instead. 'But thank you anyway.'

'Thank you,' added Aaron.

'It's my pleasure,' the man said.

Nicole felt him watching them as they left the shore and headed back towards the cottage, but by the time Ross returned home that evening she had forgotten all about him.

But Aaron hadn't. It was the first thing he told his grandfather—and Ross was furious.

'I've told you never to speak to strangers or accept anything from them,' he scolded. 'And as for you, Nicole, how could you allow it?'

She looked at him in amazement. This was surely overreacting? 'The man found my camera. I couldn't ignore him.'

'You could have stopped him giving Aaron money.'

She didn't tell him she'd thought it was an extravagance. 'It was a nice gesture,' she said instead. 'I'm sure Aaron wouldn't have spoken to him if I hadn't been there.'

Ross scowled at her. 'Make sure that it doesn't happen again.' And the conversation was dropped.

But later, in their room, as they were getting ready for bed, he brought it up again. 'I don't like strangers taking an interest in Aaron,' he said. 'It's not healthy. What was the man's name?'

'I don't know,' said Nicole, spreading her hands helplessly. 'Heavens, Ross, what's the matter with you? You're being paranoid. It was a perfectly harmless conversation. The man was very kind, actually.'

'Too kind,' he growled. 'I bet he asked Aaron's name, and how old he was, and where he lived. You can't be too careful these days.'

'As a matter of fact,' she replied, 'he did ask his name and age, but it's the sort of thing people always ask little children. Ross—' she went to him then and put her arms around him and turned her face up to him '—stop worrying. Aaron's safe with me. I look after him as if he's my own; you've nothing to fret about.'

And then she lifted her mouth to his, and he groaned, and his arms closed about her—and his lips claimed hers—and, as every night for the last week, they drowned themselves in each other's bodies.

She knew, though, how much he worried about his grandson. And she supposed it was only natural, considering all he'd been through. She made a silent vow to make sure that nothing ever happened to Aaron. She would guard him with her life.

For the next few days she and Aaron were confined to the house as Tilda was going through another bad patch and needed Nicole's constant attention. But, showing surprising resilience, she rallied again, and Nicole was able to take Aaron exploring in the estuary.

He loved messing about in water, and sometimes they went to Widemouth Bay, where they watched the windsurfers and he would clap his hands with glee whenever they fell off. 'I want to do it, I want to do it,' he'd say, and

Nicole had to promise that when he was older she would let him have a go.

One evening Ross asked Joan Steele, a neighbour, to keep an eye on Aaron and Tilda while he took Nicole out for a meal at his restaurant in Bude.

Rails was on the outskirts of the town, on a cliff road overlooking the sea, an old Edwardian building imaginatively lit and looking warm and welcoming on this chilly autumn evening.

For the occasion she'd chosen a dramatic red dress, a black cape and high-heeled black shoes. The effort had been worth it when Ross's mouth dropped open. He'd never seen her in red before—she actually didn't like herself in it, though everyone else did—and he had simply shaken his head in admiration.

'You look wonderful, Nicole, absolutely stunning. Thank you.'

She had frowned. 'What are you thanking me for?'

'Dressing up for me, making me feel honoured. Heads are going to turn tonight, I can assure you.'

And he was right. Heads did turn. Everyone who worked there wanted to take a look at Ross's new wife. In the lounge bar where they took pre-dinner drinks he introduced her to most of his team and she was conscious of their interest and approval.

But they also aroused attention when the maître d' led them to their table, and Nicole guessed that almost every lady present admired her handsome escort and wished they were in her shoes. And maybe some of the men were envying Ross too.

'Is this all right for you?' he asked as they sat down.

'It's more than all right, Ross. It's wonderful.'

'As this was my first restaurant, I have to confess that I have something of a soft spot for it.'

'I don't care whether it's your first or your last,' she said, 'it has a marvellous atmosphere.' Wood panelling and pink lampshades gave a warm, romantic glow. Potted palms and other exotic plants provided privacy, and soft music was a perfect background to the steady hum of conversation. 'What made you decide to bring me here?'

'I thought you deserved a night out,' he said with a warm, enveloping smile. 'You work hard.'

Nicole shook her head. 'It's not work. I love looking after Aaron, and your aunt's a darling. I'm just doing what any married woman would do.' *And acquiring a healthy bank balance into the bargain!*

'Yes, but it's not a normal marriage, Nicole,' he said, his expression serious. 'You must never forget that.'

Meaning that he still expected her to walk away heart-whole at the end of it. That none of their incredible love-making meant anything to him. No—it was wrong to call it lovemaking, it was sex, plain and simple sex. No emotions involved—at least not on his part. He was still in love with Alison.

It amazed her that he, or any man for that matter, could have sex—good sex—on a regular basis without wanting commitment. It was purely an affair as far as he was concerned—what he'd said it would be—and somehow it made what had become a beautiful and exciting part of her life feel incredibly sordid.

'You look sad. Is something wrong?'

What is wrong is that I think I'm falling in love with you. But she didn't say that. It was an emotion she dared not face.

'I was thinking about your aunt,' she lied, pausing a moment as their first courses were placed in front of them. In fact she was glad of the interruption, because she didn't want him to guess that his comment about theirs not being a normal marriage had upset her. 'About how much she would have enjoyed coming with us.'

Ross frowned. 'I don't think so, Nicole. She likes to be in bed early, as you well know.'

'Maybe,' she conceded. 'It just seems a shame that she's stuck in the house all the time.'

'I think you're forgetting how ill she really is.'

'I guess it's because she never complains.' Nicole spread a tiny amount of pâté on a piece of melba toast and nibbled the edge.

'She's very fond of you,' he pointed out. 'I was cross with Mark when he placed that ad, but I couldn't have chosen anyone better. I do appreciate all that you're doing for me.'

Nicole winced inwardly. She didn't want his appreciation, she wanted his love. 'It's what I'm paid for,' she said quietly.

It was his turn to look uncomfortable and he put down his fork. 'I don't want our—er—bedroom activities to be reduced to that, Nicole.'

'Why? Because it makes me sound like a whore?' She couldn't control her sudden anger, nor the words that came out. 'Maybe that's what I am? It's funny, it never occurred to me until you put it into words. What's it like to pay for sex, Ross? How does it make you feel?'

When she saw the dull red flush steal across his face she almost wished she hadn't spoken so hastily. When he'd offered the marriage contract he'd promised not to touch her. She was the one who'd encouraged him—and now she was blaming him!

But she wasn't about to back down. She tossed her head, blue eyes flashing. 'Embarrassed, are you? Suddenly realised what's happening?'

'I thought that—'

'I don't care what you think,' she thrust rashly. 'The point is—

'Nicole, Ross, what a surprise. I didn't expect to bump into you.'

Her words cut off, Nicole looked up and saw Marie smiling down at them. She changed her scowl to a smile. 'Marie, how lovely to see you. I'm sorry I haven't phoned.' She'd been meaning to ever since she'd returned from honeymoon, but somehow had never seemed to find the time. 'I've—'

'Been having the time of your life. I know; I can tell. I've never seen you look so good. Ross must be treating you well.' She flashed a cheeky glance at him as she spoke.

He inclined his head. 'I do my best.'

'What are you doing here, Marie?' Nicole knew Rails was out of her friend's league. 'Is Terri with you?'

'Terri?' Marie lifted her brows derisively. 'This place is for lovers, not girlfriends.'

'So who's your date?' Someone wealthier than her normal dating partners, that was for sure.

Marie smiled mischievously. 'Can't you guess?'

Nicole shook her head, frowning faintly. How was she supposed to know when she hadn't seen Marie for over a fortnight?

'How about you, Ross? Do you know?'

'Of course I don't,' he said, looking a little impatient that his evening was being disturbed.

'Just cast your eyes over there.'

'Mark!' Ross showed his disbelief. 'You're with Mark?'

'The very same.'

'But how? When? I had no idea.' He added accusingly, 'Mark's said nothing to me.'

Marie grinned. 'We thought we'd keep it secret for a while. I have you to thank, Ross, and you, Nicole. Mark and I met at your wedding. We've been seeing each other ever since.'

Mark raised his hand in salutation but he didn't come over, and Marie, with another pleased-for-herself grin and a whispered aside to Nicole, 'More research for the article, eh?' walked slowly and with much suggestive hip-swinging, back to her seat.

'Well,' said Ross, 'that's a surprise.'

'For me too.'

'He never said a word.'

'I should have phoned her.'

'I meant to ask you to invite both your friends over.'

'Poor Terri.'

'What do you mean?'

'She'll be on her own now.'

'Perhaps she's found a boyfriend too?'

'I hope so.' But it could mean that the trio would never be a trio again.

'What did she say to you?'

'Who?'

'Marie, of course. She whispered something before she left.'

Nicole smiled. 'Girl-talk, Ross. You wouldn't be interested.'

'You could try me.'

'I don't think so.' And she cursed Marie for arousing his curiosity. She had no intention of writing any article. It had been a non-starter from the beginning, if the truth were known, ever since she'd fallen for his indisputable charm.

'So,' he said slowly, 'what were we talking about before we were so rudely interrupted?'

Did he have to ask? She knew he hadn't forgotten, so why bring it up again when it was spoiling their evening? She shook her head. 'It wasn't important.'

'It was important enough for you to get on your high horse. I hadn't realised you felt that way. I thought you were enjoying yourself. Enjoying.' He grimaced. 'A feeble word to describe your uninhibited responses. But if that's the way you feel then rest assured I won't trouble you again.' With determination he stabbed at a mushroom and tossed it into his mouth.

Nicole wished she could put the clock back. A few careless words and she'd ruined everything. She could try apologising, but somehow she didn't think it would work. The damage had been done. So she remained silent as she ate the remainder of her pâté. Not that she wanted it now, and she didn't relish having to force her way through the rest of the meal either.

Their wine glasses were refilled, their plates whisked away, and the silence was uncomfortable and interminable. And Nicole knew that if she didn't say something soon she might as well get up and walk out.

'I'm surprised Mark didn't tell you about Marie.'

'Me too.'

'She's not usually so secretive.'

'Nor is Mark.'

Hell, this was getting them nowhere. Try something else.

'Are your other restaurants as well designed as this one?'

He smiled then, faintly—she'd touched on something dear to his heart. 'They're all different, very individual. The interior depends very much on the exterior. This is an old building so I wanted to keep it in the same period. But my St Ives restaurant, for instance, is very modern. If you like this one, if you prefer something more traditional, you might not like it, but it does well with the young professionals.'

'I'd like to see it some time.'

He looked surprised, his dark eyes making full contact with hers for the first time since their heated words.

Nicole felt the familiar flicker of her nerve-ends, a spiral of sensation lift from her stomach, and knew that whatever had been said between them nothing inside her had changed. She still wanted to share his bed.

'You're not just saying that?'

'Of course not,' she replied. 'I'm interested in everything that you do.'

His dark eyes continued to question hers, but she saw no desire leaping there. They were back to the shuttered emotions, to the control that had run his life ever since his wife and daughter died.

Her buttered fillet of salmon arrived, and Ross's steak, and their attention turned to their meal. With the tension lessened they began to talk more easily, and by the end of the evening they were almost back to normal.

Almost, but not quite. There was something missing. That vital something that had developed through their intimacy, their freedom to express their needs through the sexual act.

Marie and Mark came to their table again before leaving, and Mark looked sheepishly at Ross when he asked why he'd kept his relationship secret.

'Not so much secret, as a wish to hug my new-found feelings to myself,' replied Mark. 'But I'm glad you know. You're not the only one now, mate, to have a stunner at his side.' He looked fondly at Marie as he spoke, and then again at Ross. 'Is all well here?'

'Why shouldn't it be?' asked Ross, immediately on the defensive.

Nicole had been praying that Marie hadn't heard them arguing, now she feared that she must have, or maybe they'd looked across during the course of the evening and seen the tension between them.

'No reason, my friend,' said Mark. 'Just a figure of speech. Enjoy the rest of your meal.'

When they'd gone Ross sighed. 'This evening hasn't been the success I'd hoped.'

'I've enjoyed the food,' said Nicole, and that was the truth. Although she'd felt little like eating at one stage she had surprised herself and really tucked in to her main course. The salmon had been cooked to perfection and the unusual crackling that had accompanied it—which Ross had told her was the crisped skin of the salmon—had been an added delight.

They took their time over their coffee and brandy and it was late by the time they got home. Joan informed them that both Tilda and Aaron were fast asleep, asked if they'd had a good evening, and then hurried back to her husband.

They were alone! Bed beckoned, but Nicole was aware that sleeping together could now prove an embarrassment. Perhaps she could sneak into her old room? Ross would hardly complain and no one need know.

But it was as if he'd read her thoughts. 'Don't even think about using the other bed,' he said sternly. 'I don't want so much as a whisper to reach Tilda that something's wrong. She said only today that she was so enormously pleased I'd found someone to love again. And it has to stay that way as far as she's concerned. Understood?'

Nicole was tempted to say, *You're the one paying for the pleasure. Of course I'll do as you say.* Only she didn't. They'd reached some kind of a truce and she didn't want battle stations to start all over again. So she nodded. 'Your bed it is. I think I'll go now. Are you coming?' Her heart stopped beating as she waited for his reply.

Thankfully he shook his head. 'I'll have a drink and relax

a while, perhaps listen to some music. Goodnight, Nicole,
sleep well.'

He dipped his head and she thought he was going to kiss
her. She started to panic because, Lord help her, her need
of him was as strong as ever. But he did no more than
touch his lips to her brow.

It was enough to sear her skin, but not enough to have
her crawling all over him, begging him to come to bed and
make love to her.

The bed felt empty, and Nicole was sure she wouldn't
sleep, but she did. She slept solidly all night through, and
when she woke the next morning there was still an empty
space beside her.

She moved her leg across, then her arm—and it was ever
so slightly warm. She looked at the pillow—and it was
dented where his head had lain. Quivers of sensation closed
her throat.

He'd lain with her! Had he touched? Had he kissed? Had
he caressed? She didn't know. And she found it strange
that she hadn't sensed him, hadn't woken. Tears pricked
her eyes that it should be so.

She wanted to believe that he had touched her. She didn't
want to think that he had remained rigid the whole night
through, careful not to let their bodies make contact.

After showering and dressing she went in search of
Aaron, finding him tucked up in Tilda's bed. 'He woke
when Ross left,' said the old lady, stroking Aaron's hair
fondly. 'Ross told him not to disturb you because you'd
had a late night. Actually, you've only just missed him.
How was the meal?'

'Excellent,' said Nicole. 'It's a lovely restaurant.' Was
Ross being thoughtful, or just keeping out of her way?

'I know,' replied Tilda. 'Ross used to take me, before
my illness.'

Nicole expected him to ring her later—he usually checked on Aaron and Tilda at least once a day—and she grew increasingly irritated when she heard nothing from him.

He was taking their tiff too seriously. He had told her to act naturally and yet he was doing the exact opposite. By five o'clock, the time he usually came home, there was still no sign of him. She'd given Aaron his dinner and was preparing their own meal when Tilda wandered into the kitchen.

'It will be strange without Ross tonight. I've grown used to the three of us eating together.'

'Ross won't be here?' As usual the words were out before Nicole could stop them.

'Surely you've not forgotten?'

'Of course I haven't,' Nicole answered quickly. 'Well, at least only momentarily.' So where the devil was he? Why hadn't he told her what his plans were?

'I thought it was only me who forgot things,' said Tilda with a smile. 'He used to stay out nights regularly—until he married you. Then he couldn't tear himself away.' Tilda smiled again indulgently. 'I bet you're missing him?'

Nicole grimaced and nodded.

'Never mind. I expect he'll phone tonight. He's always wanted to open a restaurant in London. I hope he's lucky this time. He's had his eye on many properties over the years but he's always missed out.' Then Tilda laughed. 'Listen to me. You probably know all this. Take no notice. My mind rambles a lot these days.'

'It's all right,' said Nicole. 'Talk all you like.' The more she learned the less likely she was to make a fool of herself. At least she now knew where Ross was, but she still wished that he'd told her.

It was turned ten when he phoned. Tilda had gone to bed

and Nicole was curled up in an armchair watching the news on TV. 'Ross,' she said at once. 'Where the devil are you?'

'You sound panicked,' he said. 'Is everything all right?' It was a sharp question and she knew he was not thinking of her.

'No, it's damn well not all right,' she retorted. 'You could have told me that you'd be away. I felt such a fool.'

'I told Tilda,' he said woodenly. 'You have my mobile number. What's the problem?'

'I almost told her that I hadn't a clue where you were.'

'I knew you wouldn't let me down.'

'Oh, you did, did you?' she enquired indignantly. 'Pray tell me, when did you make up your mind to leave?'

'Yesterday.'

'Yet you didn't have the decency to tell me?'

There was a faint snort down the line. 'I think other things got in the way.'

So he was laying the blame on her! 'Thank you, Ross.'

'Don't mention it. How's Aaron?'

'Fine.'

'And Tilda?'

'She's fine too.'

'That's all right, then. Are you in bed?'

What if she was? It certainly didn't mean that he was imagining her there, that he was wanting her as badly as she wanted him. All that had finished. A few ill-chosen words had put paid to their love-life.

'No, I'm watching TV.'

'Oh. Good programme?'

'The news, actually.'

'I see.'

'Where are you, Ross?' Why should he ask all the questions.'

'In a hotel room.'

'Are you in bed?'

A short silence, then, 'Yes.'

Nicole closed her eyes. It was all too easy to imagine them together. She forced herself to stop it. 'How did your day go? Tilda said you were checking property.'

'That's right.'

'And?'

'It looks very promising. But so that it won't get snapped up from under my nose I'm staying overnight. I need to sort out the legalities.'

'Will you be home tomorrow?'

'Do you want me home, Nicole?'

What sort of a damn fool question was that? 'You know I do.'

'No, I don't.'

'Ross, for heaven's sake, it's you who's being funny. What I said—well, I didn't mean it. I was angry, that's all.'

'You're not a whore, Nicole,' he said quietly.

'I've never felt like one,' she admitted, her tone even huskier than it normally was. Why she'd said it she didn't know. It was another one of those occasions when she had spoken without thinking. A desire to hit back when someone upset her. Her life was full of them. They caused all sorts of complications.

'I'm glad to hear it.'

'And I'd like you in my bed tomorrow night,' she said. 'And I don't mean lying on the edge, well away from me.'

'I want that too.' His tone was gruff now, full of an emotion that he rarely let her see.

'I'll look forward to it, then.' There was a smile in her voice now. 'Goodnight, Ross.'

'Goodnight, Nicole. Think of me a little.'

'I will.' She'd think of him a lot.

'Tell Aaron I love him.'

How about telling me that you love me? An impossible dream. 'I'll tell him.'

'Bye, Nicole.'

'Bye, Ross.'

He didn't want to be the first to put down the phone. So she did it. Not that she wanted to; she wanted to talk into the night, to share emotions and needs and desires, to open their hearts and be really honest with each other. He'd never done that—and until he did, she couldn't either.

The following day Nicole felt as excited as a kitten with a ball of wool. Ross would be home. They'd made up. He would no longer shut her out. Perhaps he'd realised how much she meant to him? It was a thought she decided to hold on to.

At Aaron's insistence she took him crab-hunting, after making sure Tilda would be all right for a couple of hours. It was threatening rain but wasn't too cold, and they put on macs and wellingtons just in case.

It was as Aaron was poking at a tiny crab in one of the rock pools that Tilda saw the man again. He was watching them, and when she looked at him he raised his hand in salute and walked over.

'Hello, again.'

Aware of Ross's anger the last time they'd spoken, she acknowledged him but didn't smile, hoping that perhaps he'd go away. Not that she felt threatened by him. He was honest-looking, wore jeans, an Aran turtle-necked sweater and a navy padded jacket. He looked reasonably well off, he spoke well—nothing to fear from him. But she knew that appearances could be deceptive, and she needed to be on her guard for Aaron's sake.

Aaron also looked up and smiled shyly, but he took Nicole's hand.

'What are you doing, young man?'

'Crabs,' said Aaron, pointing.

The man stooped down to his level and looked into the pool. 'Two of them. Are you going to catch them and take them home?'

Aaron shook his head.

'You're just playing with them?'

Aaron nodded.

'Well, Aaron, I know where there's a pool with a lot more crabs.'

Alarm bells rang in Nicole's head. 'I think it's time we went home, Aaron,' she said, endeavouring to keep her voice calm. Mustn't let her fears communicate themselves to the boy.

'But, Nicole.' He looked at her with his big brown eyes. 'I want to see more crabs.'

'I mean no harm.' The man put his hands up, palms facing her, and Nicole noticed that he wore a wedding ring.

Somehow it made her feel faintly better, and she would have liked to ask whether he had children of his own, but she didn't want to start that sort of conversation.

'Very well.' But she kept Aaron's hand tightly locked in hers as they crossed the sand to the far side of the estuary.

Aaron was so excited when he saw all the crabs that he couldn't keep still. He jigged up and down and then touched one gingerly, before withdrawing his hand in case he got nipped. 'Will they go back to sea?' he asked.

The man answered. 'Sure, when the tide comes in.'

'Can I watch?'

'Afraid not. You'd get too wet. Can you swim, Aaron?'

Aaron nodded his head emphatically.

'With his water wings on,' Nicole informed him, 'but he loves the water. Do you come to the beach often, Mr— er—'

'It's Matt—call me Matt. Not as often as I'd like. I'm

on sick leave at the moment, recovering from pneumonia. I'm staying with my mother in Bude. I love the sea air. I love the water—everything connected with it. I miss it.'

'You're not a local?' She thought she detected a slight Cornish accent.

'I was born and bred in Cornwall, though I don't live here any more. You say Aaron's not your child. Are you his nanny or something?'

Nicole nodded. She was the 'or something'.

'His mother works, I suppose? Such a pity. She's missing out on his best years.' He looked thoughtfully down at Aaron as he spoke.

'His mother's dead.' Nicole saw no harm in telling him that.

'Oh!'

It was a strange 'oh'. As though he really felt something. A deep sympathy, perhaps. And yet he didn't know them. She warmed even more towards him.

'I'm sorry to hear it,' he said. 'What happened?'

'A car accident. I think it's time we went.' She'd said enough. And even as she spoke it began to rain. 'Aaron, come along.'

He was reluctant, but he obeyed.

'Perhaps we'll meet again,' said Matt.

'How long are you here for?'

'A further two weeks.'

'Well, who knows?' she said lightly. But it might be best if she kept away. Ross wouldn't be very pleased if he found out that she and his precious grandson were still talking to the stranger.

Actually, he no longer felt like a stranger. He had a name now, and he was pleasant and well-mannered and seemed genuine enough. She looked back and saw him walking away in the opposite direction, hands shoved into his pockets, head bowed against the now teeming rain.

They ran into the cottage, laughing as they shrugged off their macs and kicked off their wellies, and Nicole went to see if Tilda was in need of anything, Aaron in tow.

'My, you look as though you've had a good time,' the woman said, looking at their damp shining faces.

'We saw crabs,' said Aaron importantly. 'Lots of them.' And he spread his arms wide. 'The man showed us.'

'What man?' asked Tilda, only mildly curious.

'The money man.'

Tilda frowned. 'What's he talking about?'

'It's someone we met on the beach the other day,' laughed Nicole. 'He gave Aaron some money for sweets. He was there again. The poor man's convalescing from pneumonia. I think he needed someone to talk to.'

'But it didn't have to be you—or Aaron.' Ross's voice sounded like thunder behind her.

'Ross!' She couldn't disguise her pleasure, although it was tinged with dismay that he'd walked in at this exact moment. She'd been looking forward to him coming, had envisaged a warm welcome, a hug, a kiss. And now he was looking at her as though she'd committed a heinous crime.

CHAPTER EIGHT

'YOU deliberately went against my wishes.' Ross had led Nicole up to their bedroom, where they could talk without being overheard. 'You know how much I disapproved of you speaking to him.'

'What was I supposed to do? Ignore him?' she asked. 'Like I said before, Ross, you're worrying for nothing. He just wanted someone to speak to. He's at a loose end; he's convalescing.'

'Really?' he sneered. 'It looks as though you had quite a conversation.'

'No, I didn't. Don't be so unreasonable.' She was trying hard not to lose her temper but it was difficult in the face of Ross's disapproval. She'd had such high hopes for when he came home, and now everything was once more crumbling at her feet.

'I expect you exchanged names, and arranged to meet again?' he asked accusingly.

He was jealous! That was it! Nicole gave an inward smile. It wasn't so much that he was worried about Aaron; he thought that *she* was interested in this man.

'Of course not,' she said quickly now. 'Why should I want to see him again?'

'So you didn't find out his name?'

'As a matter of fact, yes, I did. It's Matt.'

'Matt?' His eyes narrowed. 'Matt who?' he asked sharply.

Too sharply, she thought. 'I don't know,' she answered testily. 'Why does it matter? What is this? The third degree?'

'What did he look like? How old is he?' He completely ignored her questions.

Nicole shrugged expressively, unable to understand why he was bombarding her with questions. 'Gosh, Ross, why's it so important? Early twenties, I suppose. Blond, good-looking, about your height.'

'A scar on his cheek?'

'For heaven's sake, I don't know.' And then, 'Well, yes, I think there was a faint one. I didn't really take much notice. I—'

She jumped when Ross slammed a fist into his palm. 'Dammit, I knew it was him.' And he slammed it again, and again.

Nicole looked at him apprehensively, just a little bit scared. 'Knew it was who?'

'Who? *Who?*' he repeated, eyes blazing. 'Do you need to ask? The one man who can take Aaron from me. Haven't you got it yet? It's Aaron's father.'

Ross had always known the day would come when Matt Cooper turned up again and demanded he hand over Aaron. It was his worst nightmare. Something he had feared from the day his darling Tara had died.

He should have officially adopted his grandson, he knew, but that would have meant tracing Matt, and it was something he'd been reluctant to do in case the younger man decided he wanted the boy after all. This incident now proved how right he'd been to worry.

'How can you be sure it's him?' asked Nicole. 'I only gave you a vague description.'

'I'm sure,' Ross replied with conviction.

'You know him well?'

'I don't know him at all,' he answered cryptically, 'and I damn well don't want to. He hurt my Tara and he sure as hell is not going to take what I've got left of her.'

'But if he's Aaron's father surely he has the right to see him?' she asked reasonably.

'Dammit, Nicole, you don't know what you're talking about.'

Perhaps he should tell her. She deserved that much at least. He sat down heavily on the edge of the bed and dropped his head in his hands.

'Ross.' Her voice was persuasive, concerned, and she touched her hand to his shoulder.

In that moment he wanted nothing more than to take her into his arms and let her put everything right. She had done just that for a few magical nights. She'd made him forget the unhappiness that haunted him and almost promised a future. Except that he knew he dared not take advantage of that promise. Fate would intercede once again if he did.

So he knocked her arm away. 'Matt Cooper made my daughter pregnant,' he said bitterly. 'She came home from university one day in tears. He was her boyfriend at the time, but when she told him that she was carrying his baby he didn't want to know, even said it might not be his. But she assured me there'd been no one else. I tried to get his name out of her but she wasn't telling. Perhaps as well, because I'd probably have killed him.'

He drew in a deep breath through flared nostrils, held it a moment, and then let it out on a violent shudder.

'So you've never met him before?'

'Oh, yes, I've met him,' he answered grimly. 'Aaron was a few months old when Tara finally told me his name. She didn't mean to, it slipped out, and I never told her that I went to see him. He was a fellow student. I warned him that if he ever came anywhere near Tara or her son his life wouldn't be worth living—*if* he lived. I thought he'd got the message. Obviously not.'

'You're not going to do anything silly?' asked Nicole, sounding alarmed.

'If you mean am I going to kill him? No. It would never have got that far but, God, was I angry. I'd always dreamed about Tara getting married in white, a big church wedding, a honeymoon in the Caribbean, a few years enjoying herself before she finally started a family. And that damn man ruined it. I wanted so much for her, a better start than Alison and I ever had.'

'I'm so sorry,' said Nicole quietly. 'I didn't realise. You never talked about Tara. I—'

'Because it hurts. It still hurts, dammit. I was a fool to think that...' He shook his head. He'd been about to say that she'd been helping him get over it. It was wishful thinking. No one could do that. His life was mapped out. Pain and torment was his cross to bear for evermore.

'It's time to go back home, Nicole.'

He saw her frown, the way it made two delicate little furrows between her brows that he wanted to kiss away. But never again. He must not, must never, let himself get too close to her, too fond of her.

'I'm sorry,' she said. 'I'm not with you?'

'Of course. I didn't explain, did I? This isn't my permanent home.'

'Oh?'

He could see the puzzlement on her face. 'It used to be, when we first moved down here—at least half of it was, until we bought the other cottage and knocked it into one. But when the business took off Alison wanted something grander and we bought a house in Exeter. It's spacious and elegant and Alison loved it.

'This became our holiday retreat, somewhere we could hide when we needed to recharge our batteries. When Aaron started to walk Tara thought it would be better for him if they lived here. Tilda came with her. Alison and I stayed at Court House. When Tara died I thought it best not to uproot Aaron. He was lost enough without his mother. So I moved in as well.'

'You've been here ever since?'

'Yes.'

'And you really think it's a good idea to move back to Exeter now? Aaron will be devastated. He loves the sea; you know he does.'

'It's within easy driving distance,' he said dismissively, while knowing that what she said made sense.

'But that's not the same. It's on his doorstep here. He can walk out of the cottage and virtually on to the beach. He absolutely adores exploring. What would he do in Exeter? When he starts school then maybe, yes, you can move him, but I don't think you should now.'

She looked really concerned and he admired her for it. But there was one major concern she seemed to have overlooked. 'You're forgetting Matt,' he reminded her tersely.

'No, I'm not,' she assured him. 'He's only here for another two weeks, then he'll be gone again. I'm sure there's nothing sinister about him being here. He's had pneumonia and he's living with his mother for a while; he thought the sea air would do him good. I think he's married as well; he's wearing a ring.'

'My, my, quite the little detective,' he couldn't help sneering. But it hurt that she'd noticed, that she'd found out so much in such a short space of time. Matt was an attractive man, he had to grudgingly admit, a woman's man. It had drawn Tara to him, and now even Nicole seemed hooked. 'I suppose you found out where he lives as well?'

Nicole looked hurt, as well she might, but he refused to apologise.

'No, I didn't, as a matter of fact,' she answered. 'I asked no questions. Whatever he told me was voluntary. And I still think you're being over-suspicious. Why don't I keep

Aaron away from St Meek for the next couple of weeks? I can take him to Padstow, he'll love the boats there, and Tintagel, to see King Arthur's castle, and he adores watching the windsurfers at Bude and Widemouth Bay. Then there's—'

He held up his hand. 'OK, OK, you've convinced me.' Even though it was against his better judgement. 'You must promise me, though, that you'll never let Aaron out of your sight until you're sure that Matt's gone, and you'll never put him in any danger whatsoever.' He felt like a monster, extracting this promise, but if he lost Aaron now then he would have lost everything.

'I promise,' she said seriously, and stuck up the middle three fingers of her right hand. 'Guide's honour.'

She looked so appealing that he wanted to take her into his arms and cuddle her, but he knew that would lead to dangerous ground. And yet...

The impulse was too strong, the need too strong. He pushed himself up and she was ready for him. Their arms locked around each other, their mouths came together, and she wove her magic over him.

He was able to forget his fear, forget that Matt might have come to claim Aaron, forget everything except this sweet-smelling woman he held in his arms. Desire pulsed through his veins, and although he knew it was wrong to take what she so willingly gave when he could offer nothing in return, he hadn't the strength to put a stop to it.

It was like drinking the ambrosia of life. She filled him with warmth and happiness, with pleasure, with a gut-wrenching need to make love to her right here and now.

He heard himself groan, knew he was crushing her too hard against him, but she didn't complain, and when he began to peel off her sweater with trembling hands she didn't resist. In fact she helped.

And when she stood before him completely naked she

began undressing him, snapping buttons off his shirt in her
haste, letting him unfasten his belt buckle because it was
awkward, but then unzipping his trousers herself and letting
them fall at his feet where he kicked them free. His briefs
followed. His manhood stood proudly erect.

He was lost. He was hers; she was his. She ran her fingers lightly over his chest, tweaking his nipples, sending
sensation after sensation reeling through him. Then she
lowered her head and kissed his nipples. She nipped them
with her fine white teeth, and his need for her increased a
hundredfold. He wanted her to run her hands down his
body, lower, lower, to assuage this terrible ache. But she
stopped, and she smiled.

'It's your turn to kiss me now,' she said huskily.

Oh, that voice, what it did to him. He needed no second
bidding. He took her breasts between his palms in almost
humble supplication, and he kissed and he sucked and he
drank the sweetness of her. She moaned as he had moaned
earlier; she threw back her head and enjoyed. He felt the
hammer-beat of her heart, the heat of her skin, the tremors
that shivered through her, and he knew that it was going
to be impossible to keep her at arm's length.

Last night in an impersonal hotel bed he'd longed for
her, ached for her, dreamt about her, missed her. And the
night before, when he'd deliberately not touched, had carefully lain on the very edge of the bed, sleeping only inter-
mittently, it had been the worst torture imaginable—even
though it had been self-imposed.

He wasn't in love with her, but, Lord, he loved her body,
and one taste had been enough to hook him. She was like
a drug that he couldn't get enough of. Denial was out of
the question, especially as she was one very eager young
lady.

He did wonder, briefly, whether she would be hurt when
their contract finished. On the other hand she knew the

score. She was entering into it with her eyes open. Why deny her what she obviously wanted?

The excuse satisfied him, and he swept her up in his arms and laid her down on the bed. There he began to kiss every inch of her, and stroke every inch, delighting in the jerky responses, in the way she touched and clung to him, in her uninhibited cries of mounting pleasure.

She was hot and ready and he lowered himself over her—and in the distance he heard Aaron calling him.

Damn!

Nicole heard too, and he sensed her disappointment.

But they mustn't let Aaron find them like this. His grandson was prone to bursting into rooms and there'd never been any reason for Ross to stop him—until now!

'I'm sorry, Nicole,' he said gruffly.

'It's not your fault,' she whispered.

'We'll carry on with this later.'

'I'd like that.'

Like lightning they both whipped on their clothes, laughing at each other's antics, and when Aaron finally erupted on the scene they were fully dressed, though rather red-faced from the exertion.

'Grandpa, Grandpa, Tilda wants you.'

'And what does she want me for?' Ross stooped down to the boy's level, and thanked God his grandson wasn't old enough to sense what they'd been doing.

'Don't know.'

'Let's go and find out, then.' He took Aaron's hand, looking back over his shoulder as they left the room to mouth another, 'I'm sorry.'

Nicole flashed him a mischievous smile. 'We'll finish our game later, Ross.'

'What game, Grandpa?' Aaron asked. 'Can I play?'

Life was perfect, thought Nicole a few days later as she bathed Aaron before putting him to bed. She and Ross were closer than they'd ever been and the future looked promising. Surely no man could make love the way Ross did, treat her the way he did, and then dump her when she'd finished being useful? It wasn't possible.

She had been careful to keep Aaron away from his beloved rock pools and he loved the different places they visited, new sights to see, new things to do, and each evening he regaled his grandfather and Tilda with tales of his adventures.

Although Ross never mentioned Matt again, she couldn't fail to notice his careful questioning of his grandson: whether they'd met anyone, who he'd spoken to, who Nicole had spoken to. Cunning, she thought, but he needn't have worried. She'd run a million miles if she saw Matt. She wanted nothing, simply nothing, to spoil things between them.

In nearby Bude one day they watched a lone windsurfer, and afterwards walked back to the town and went into a café. Aaron was thirsty and wanted a milkshake, and she ordered a cappuccino for herself. Aaron loved cafés. It was probably an excuse that he wanted a drink, she decided as he played with his straw. There was simply something about the noise and the bustle that excited him.

Ross was in London on this particular day, finalising his deal, over which he was very enthusiastic. Nicole was pleased for him, but hoped it wouldn't take him away from home too often.

It shouldn't matter, she knew. It was wrong to lose sight of the fact that he was paying her to look after Tilda and Aaron. The fact that they had a love-life together was a bonus, and she must remember that.

Oh, no! She said the words silently but they thumped loud in her head. Matt had just entered with an older woman whom she presumed to be his mother. He hadn't seen her yet, and she wondered if they could sneak out while he was at the counter.

She hadn't considered Aaron. 'Look, Nicole, look,' he said loudly, pointing a finger. 'The money man.'

'Shh, darling,' she said immediately, but too late. Matt turned and saw them, and smiled, and immediately came over.

'I wondered where you'd got to,' he said cheerfully. 'I haven't seen you for ages.'

Nicole's returning smile was weak. 'I guess we just missed each other.' She prayed he'd leave them alone. But no such luck.

'You must meet my mother,' he said. 'I've told her all about you and Aaron.'

Her heart gave a great surge in her breast and she panicked. He'd told her *everything*? The woman knew that Aaron was her grandson! This was getting worse by the minute. 'I—I'm sorry, we—we don't really have time,' she said breathlessly, urgently. 'We have to get back and make lunch for—'

'You can spare just a minute, surely?' He looked down at their hardly touched drinks and must have known that she was lying. Had her panicky reaction given her away? Told him that she knew who he was? Or was she worrying for nothing?

He couldn't possibly know that Ross had guessed his identity and told her to keep away. She was being paranoid—the same thing that she'd accused Ross of. She forced a wider smile. 'Of course.'

He beckoned his mother and she came across. A woman who looked nothing like Matt. She was tiny, with a prematurely aged skin, greying hair, and bright blue eyes that looked piercingly at Aaron. 'Mother, this is the lady I told you about—the one I met on the beach—and this is her charge, Aaron.'

Nicole held out her hand to the woman, but it was clear that it was only the boy she was interested in. Her fears increased.

Mrs Cooper sat down and started chatting to Aaron while Matt got their teas and brought them to the table. 'We may as well join you,' he said easily.

Nicole kept her eye on Aaron and the woman, and to her dismay she produced some sweets out of her bag and gave them to him. It was clear to see that Aaron liked her.

'I don't think you should eat those,' she said, more sharply than she'd intended. 'You won't eat your lunch. We're going home in a minute.'

'Don't want to.' His little face grew red and Nicole could see that he was working himself up to do battle. It wasn't often he did, and she rarely let him have his own way, but she didn't want to create a scene in front of Matt and his mother.

'Tilda's hungry; she's waiting for us,' she reasoned.

'Tilda can make her own meal.'

'You know she can't, darling.' It was one of the aunt's off days, and Nicole had promised that she wouldn't be out long. It was why they'd gone to Bude instead of somewhere further afield.

'Who's Tilda?' asked Mrs Cooper with interest.

'Aaron's great-great-aunt. She lives with us; she's not well.'

'I see. In that case, little boy, you must go home. Take your sweets with you and maybe we'll see you again another day?'

'Tomorrow?' asked Aaron eagerly.

'We'll see,' said Nicole. And to Matt and his mother, 'I can't promise anything.'

'Of course, I understand,' said Mrs Cooper, still not taking her eyes off Aaron.

It gave Nicole an uneasy feeling. It was a weird situation.

This was the woman's grandchild, after all, and she wasn't being allowed to acknowledge it. She felt sorry for her. 'Do you have grandchildren?' she asked, then wished she hadn't when the woman's face grew sad.

She looked up at Matt and then, as though she'd been primed, said, 'No. It's my one regret.'

'There's time.'

'Of course.'

'We must go. Come along, Aaron.'

To her relief he finished his milkshake and jumped down from the chair. 'See you tomorrow,' he said brightly, and then tucked his hand into hers.

Outside the café Nicole took a few deep breaths. Somehow she had to keep this from Ross.

CHAPTER NINE

LUCK was on Nicole's side. Ross phoned early evening to say that he was staying in London overnight, maybe even for two nights, which would, she hoped, give Aaron time to forget about their meeting with Matt's mother. She didn't want to tell him to say nothing, because it was wrong to encourage him to keep secrets from his grandfather, but on the other hand she didn't want him blabbing it out and getting her into trouble again.

Nicole knew that she was going to miss Ross, hated him being away, but on this occasion she really did feel it was for the best. He phoned again later, when she was in bed, and his voice was low and sexy and sent every one of her nerve-endings into spasm.

'Where are you?' she wanted to know, aware that her own voice was also huskier than usual.

'Do you need to ask? I'm in bed, and I can't sleep for thinking about you.'

'Me too,' she whispered, her heart pounding just that little bit faster.

'I'm missing you.'

This was quite an admission, and it pleased her enormously, but before she could respond he spoke again.

'Are you missing me?'

It was the first leading question he'd ever asked and Nicole felt intensely comforted. It was yet another step in the right direction. With a bit of luck by the end of her stay here he might discover that he couldn't live without her.

When she finally snuggled down to sleep she hugged the

thought to her, and woke the next morning feeling on top of the world.

Tilda wasn't well again, and it was raining heavily so Aaron was forced to stay indoors. He wasn't happy because he was a real outdoor child, but he settled down in Tilda's room with his crayons and a colouring book while Nicole busied herself with some housework.

She'd just decided that she'd earned a rest when the doorbell rang. To her delight it was Marie. 'Guess what?' her friend said, even before she'd set foot inside the cottage. 'Mark and I are getting married.'

Nicole beamed. 'That's wonderful. I'm so pleased for you. Come in, do. But—isn't it rather sudden? You've hardly had time to get to know each other.'

'You married Ross in even less time,' Marie pointed out as Nicole closed the door behind them.

'Yes, but that was different. Ours is a marriage of convenience; there's no love involved.' *Liar!* 'I shall be free of him once my job's finished,' she added blithely. Her spine felt like a shaft of ice. Ross had become so much a part of her life that she couldn't face the thought of a future without him.

'And do you want that?' asked Marie.

Nicole frowned. 'What do you mean, do I want it? It's in my contract; I have no choice.'

'Of course you have a choice,' her friend retorted. 'Contracts can be broken. You love the guy, don't you?'

Nicole stared at Marie. 'What do you mean?'

'Come on, don't play innocent with me; I know you too well. It might have started off as a temporary assignment, but I was telling Terri only the other day that I thought your marriage was turning into a real one. Think what a terrific ending that will make to your story. Wow, I can't wait to read it.'

Nicole groaned inwardly. 'Marie, I'm not—'

But Marie wasn't listening. 'It is, isn't it? Turning into a real marriage? It's easy to see that Ross's crazy about you. Mark says he never stops talking about you, says that you're the best thing that's happened to him in a long time.'

'A cup of coffee, Marie?' Nicole needed time to digest this piece of information. *Ross kept talking about her!* Was it a hopeful sign? Did it mean what she wanted it to mean?

'I thought you'd never ask. Where is everyone, by the way? This place is like a morgue.'

'Aunt Tilda's in bed, she's having a bad day, and Aaron's with her. You know what they say about the old and the young getting on well together. Well, it's true. They just love each other's company.'

'That's good. It leaves you and Ross with more time to yourselves. Is he at work?'

'He's in London,' Nicole answered as she filled the kettle. 'He's thinking of opening a restaurant there.'

'Is that a good idea?'

She switched the kettle on then turned around. 'What do you mean?'

'Well, won't he be spending a lot of time there?'

'I suppose so, until it's up and running.'

'Won't you mind?'

Of course she minded, but she wasn't going to tell Marie that. There were some things it was best her friend didn't know. She had too ready a tongue. 'I'm being paid to look after Tilda and Aaron. What he does is no business of mine.'

'No, you're not.'

'Not what?'

'Not being paid to look after them. Ross advertised for a wife. Not a nanny, not a home help, not a nurse—a wife. I admire the way you've taken the rest of it on board, but it's not the issue.'

'I think it is.' Nicole reached out mugs and milk. 'He couldn't cope; he needed help.'

'For himself, yes. He needed someone for himself. He's had a hard time. Goodness, Nicole, if all he'd wanted was a carer for Aaron and Tilda then he'd have paid someone to do just that. He wouldn't have wanted her in his bed.'

Nicole frowned and felt herself blushing. 'How do you know we're sharing a bed?'

'How do I know the sky is blue? How do I know that grass is green? My dear Nicole, you have a glow about you that was never there before. Not even when you thought you were in love with that Bart guy.'

'Bertram.'

'Well, whoever. It shines out of you like a beacon. You're in love, girl, and if you're not sharing Ross's bed then I'm a Dutchman.'

'It's so obvious?' asked Nicole with a final sigh.

'Like the nose on my face. So, back to what we were talking about. What will you do if he decides to spend time in London?'

'Short of taking Aaron and Tilda with me, there's nothing I can do,' Nicole answered, but she hoped it wouldn't come to that. The kettle boiled. She made their coffee, and they took it with a plate of biscuits into the living room.

Aaron must have heard them talking, because he came to investigate and dived into the biscuits. Any sort of private conversation after that was out of the question.

Eventually Marie left, with the promise that she would come again soon and bring Terri with her.

Nicole couldn't wait now for Ross to return. Marie's declaration that he never stopped talking to Mark about her was good news indeed. Perhaps, despite everything, he was falling in love! He'd actually admitted that he was missing her—so, adding the two things together made the future suddenly look very rosy indeed.

And although he'd said that he might be away for two
nights he turned up just as she was putting Aaron to bed.
His grandson whooped with delight and Nicole felt like
doing the same thing. And when Ross looked at her there
was promise in his eyes, although he said nothing in front
of Aaron.

They spent time with Tilda and then sat either side of
the log fire and talked. They talked about his new restaurant, they talked about Aaron, and how quickly he was
growing up, they talked about Tilda and the fact that she
seemed to be having more and more off days. But they
didn't talk about themselves.

Nicole told Ross about Marie's visit. She wanted to tell
him what her friend had said, but she was afraid that if she
did he might back off. He probably didn't realise that he'd
given himself away.

They drank hot chocolate, their mugs cupped in their
hands, their eyes frequently meeting and then darting away
again. Nicole's pulses were racing. She didn't know what
to expect.

'Come here,' he said finally, when she'd almost given
up, when she'd begun to fear that he'd had second thoughts
about continuing their relationship.

Slowly she rose and crossed the few short feet that sep-
arated them. When she was standing in front of him he
pulled her down on to his lap. And he groaned as his arms
tightened around her. 'I never thought I'd hear myself say
this,' he said, 'but you've become a part of my life, Nicole.'

Hope rose within her, soaring like a bird on the wing.

'I cannot imagine it without you.'

Higher and higher it flew.

'But you know that's impossible? You know that I can
offer you nothing?'

And dropped again just as suddenly. She heard the thud
as it fell to the floor, to lie there in disillusioned fragments.

'But let's not think about that now. I want you, Nicole. Oh, Lord, I want you.' His mouth sought hers and although she knew that she ought to deny him, that it was pointless carrying on when the future was non-existent, she somehow couldn't help herself.

Her lips parted of their own accord, his tongue probed and sent pulse racing. His hand cupped her breast and it burgeoned beneath his palm, nipple tingling with excitement as his thumb stroked and incited.

'You're an incredible woman,' he said, his voice low and husky and filled with an emotion she knew he didn't welcome but which he couldn't deny.

Nicole didn't answer. She wanted to pay him compliments too, but was afraid that if she did he might back off. After what he'd said she feared to show her feelings in case he felt she was becoming too serious.

His hands trembled slightly, as though he was having difficulty in hiding his urgent need of her. 'You arouse new and wondrous feelings inside me. I can't help myself when you're around.'

'That's all right,' she whispered, her throat aching with a very real need. Everything was all right. She refused to dwell on what her future held. Best to grab each opportunity as it came.

She knew now without a shadow of a doubt that she was in love with Ross Dufrais. So why deny herself the pleasure he was offering? So long as she never lost sight of the fact that it wasn't a permanent relationship there was no reason why she couldn't enjoy herself and walk away at the end of it. *And who was she trying to kid?*

On the other hand if she rejected Ross, if she denied him her body, then her time here would be sheer hell. Which did she prefer? There was really no choice.

Her hand slid inside the open neck of his shirt, over the warm firmness of his skin, and the contact made her gasp.

She clung, and she moaned, and she searched again for his mouth.

Ross seemed to go a little crazy too, tearing at her top until her breasts were exposed to his greedy eyes—and his hands, and his mouth. 'Let's go to bed,' he said thickly.

'Let's do it here,' Nicole insisted.

He didn't hesitate. Clothes were hastily disposed of and Nicole knew that she would never look again at the woollen rug in front of the fire without remembering this moment.

As they lay there he stroked and kissed every inch of her. He ignited her in ways she'd never imagined possible, until her spine was arching, her hands clawing, and her breathing grew deep and unsteady. 'Take me,' she urged. 'Take me now.'

He needed no second bidding, but he had hardly entered her when Nicole felt a wild climactic surge that sent her body into spasm and her heart into overtime. She clutched and clawed as wave after intense wave flooded through her, filling her whole body with mind-blowing sensation, and when he too lost control, when the same wild pressure exploded inside him, she held him as though she never wanted to let him go.

It had never been like this with Alison, thought Ross. He'd never doubted for one moment the depth of his love for his wife, or hers for him. But Alison had been very conservative when it came to making love. In bed and with the light off.

She'd never disappointed him, never turned him away, but occasionally, just occasionally, he'd wished for something more, wished she would take the initiative—and then had chastised himself for being selfish.

Nicole, on the other hand, had no inhibitions. Making love was a pure joy to her: any time, any place, it seemed, which suited him down to the ground. And he was beginning to wish, just a little bit, that he hadn't set any ground rules.

It was going to be difficult to let her go, but he knew that he must. He knew he dared not let her, or anyone else for that matter, into his life or he would inevitably lose her. So he made himself believe that he wasn't in love with Nicole, that it was pure lust, a physical need. And that it would burn itself out eventually and then it would be easy to let her go.

For the moment, though, he needed her, and he needed her badly. Now! Again! She lay on her back at his side, her eyes closed, a satisfied smile on her lips. One hand was beneath her head, the other resting idly on his thigh, and the flickering light from the log fire accentuated every soft feminine curve of her delightful body. She was so beautiful, and, Lord, how he wanted her.

He turned so that her hand made contact with his life force. He felt the blood surging in him again at her touch as her fingers closed around him, and he gave a deep-throated groan. 'More,' he urged. 'I want more.'

'You're insatiable, do you know that?' she teased as she continued to torment.

'Is that the pot calling the kettle black?'

'Not at all,' she said with pretended indignance. 'I'm merely answering your demands.' And then she leaned over him and touched and stroked with the tip of her tongue, tasted and pleasured, increasing his agony, nearly driving him out of his mind.

'You little witch,' he growled, and, impatient now, he parted her thighs and lowered himself over her and into her. And even though only a few scant minutes had passed since the last time, even though he should have lasted a whole lot longer, he didn't. And he felt uncomfortable by it.

'I'm sorry,' he muttered thickly.

'What for?'

'I didn't mean to—'

'Don't!' she told him, putting her finger to his lips. 'I love it. It gives me a great feeling of power.'

'It does?' This was something that had never occurred to him. Alison had always lain silent after making love, curled up away from him and gone to sleep. This declaration of feelings was a new experience—and he liked it.

'I love the feeling that I can make you lose control so easily.'

'You little minx. I'll show you.'

And he took her again, and this time he made it last, until she was the one to cry out, to thrash and groan beneath him, to give vent to the intense sensations that he knew were exploding within her.

Finally they were both sated. Finally he suggested they needed a drink. And finally they made their way up to bed.

He slept like a newborn baby, but the next morning hunger surged in him again and he made love to her before he went to work, loving the fact that Nicole seemed equally as insatiable.

Mark took one look at him when he arrived and said knowingly, 'It's easy to see what sort of night you've had.'

'And pray what might that be?' he asked, trying to pretend that he didn't know what his partner was talking about.

'Sex, my good friend, and plenty of it. Glad to see my little scheme's worked out.'

'Sex doesn't mean I'm in love with the woman,' he retorted, irritated by Mark's flippant attitude.

'Really?'

'Yes, really! I shall still let her go when the time comes.' Even though he knew now that it would be hard, and that the longer she remained in his life the more difficult it would become, if not impossible.

'Then you're a fool,' Mark scorned. 'She's perfect. She fulfils your every need. Can you deny that?'

Ross shrugged, trying to appear nonchalant. 'She's proved an asset, yes, but once Tilda—'

'Rubbish,' the other man cut in impatiently. 'Your venerable aunt has nothing to do with it.'

Ross shook his head vehemently. 'You're wrong there, my friend. Tilda has everything to do with my getting married. I did it for her sake.'

'So you told yourself. So you told Nicole. And maybe it's what you thought you wanted in the beginning.' Mark eyed his colleague, an eyebrow raised in speculation. 'But things have changed between you and your beautiful wife. She means something to you now. She's got beneath your skin, and you'd be insane to give her up.'

Ross shook his head sadly and heaved a sigh. 'You're right, but you also know how ill-fated I am. I can't afford to take the risk.' It made him sound foolish, he knew. Why shouldn't he snatch some happiness while he could? But he had Nicole to think of too. He musn't put her life at risk.

'Ross, Ross,' urged his friend, 'don't talk like that. I know you've had more than your fair share of tragedy, but the fates wouldn't be so unkind as to heap even more on you.

'Listen to Uncle Mark. This woman is meant for you. I think you're even happier with her than you were with Alison—not that you didn't love her,' he added quickly, with a forestalling lift of his hand, 'I know you did and that you always will. But there are different kinds of love. Nicole's a very different kind of girl. You're made for each other.' Then he shook his head. 'I know that sounds trite, but I actually happen to think it's true. I've seen such a difference in you since she came into your life.'

'Don't you think it's too good to last?' A few minutes

ago Ross would have definitely said, It's too good to last. He was surprised to recognize that Mark was talking sense.

'No, I don't, my friend. In this life you have to grab each opportunity as it comes. You're not jinxed. It wasn't your fault that your parents died young.'

'Well, no, but—'

'Or that Alison and—'

'Yes, that *was* my fault,' Ross cut in swiftly, loudly, angrily. 'No one can say otherwise.'

'No, no, no,' said Mark, equally as firmly. 'It was an accident, a pure and simple accident. It could have happened to anyone. You just happened to be in the wrong place at the wrong time.'

'There was nothing simple about it,' Ross retorted. 'I didn't react quickly enough. Maybe I only delayed a second in recognising that we were heading for the truck, but it was enough to cost them their lives.'

Mark had been with him through the trauma, and he clapped his hand on Ross's shoulder now. 'Don't torture yourself. Something good's finally happening to you. Accept it, enjoy it, make the most of it.'

Ross decided it was time to change the subject. 'I hear you're getting married yourself?'

Mark beamed. 'Indeed I am. Marie's a treasure. She's so full of life, so funny, so sexy, so everything. I'm going to make her mine before someone else snaps her up.'

'I'm pleased for you.'

'As I am pleased for you. Don't forget what I said. No negative thoughts.'

As the morning wore on and Ross thought over their conversation he began to see the truth in what Mark had said. Why shouldn't he turn their marriage into a proper one? Providing Nicole was agreeable, of course. Why should he continue torturing himself when he was being offered another chance of happiness? He felt almost certain that Nicole was falling in love with him. And if she wasn't it wouldn't be long before she did.

In fact he was almost bubbling with happiness when he drove home. He didn't often go home for lunch now that he had Nicole to look after Aaron and Tilda, but today he was eager to see her. He wanted to make love to her again. He wanted to make up for all the months he'd remained celibate.

But his happiness turned to alarm when he was met at the door by an almost demented Nicole. 'Oh, Ross, Ross, I was just going to ring you. Aaron's gone missing.'

CHAPTER TEN

'WHAT do you mean,' Ross yelled, 'he's gone missing? How? When? Why didn't you keep your eye on him?' It was happening again. Just when he thought he'd been given a new chance fate had decreed otherwise. He should have known better. He clapped his hands to his head. Please, God, let his grandson be safe. *Please.*

'We were playing outside,' Nicole explained, wringing her hands in despair, her face deathly white. 'I heard Tilda calling. I only left him for a couple of minutes.'

'Damn you!' he roared. 'You shouldn't have left him at all. You should have taken him inside with you.'

'I didn't know that—'

'I don't want your excuses, dammit. Where have you looked? What have you done about it? Have you phoned the police?'

'Not yet. I—'

'Why the hell not?' He no longer felt like making love to her; he was disappointed in her. He'd trusted her, he'd felt that Aaron was safe with her, and now she'd let him down.

'It's only just happened.'

'Then he can't have gone far.'

'I've searched everywhere I can think of,' she told him thinly. 'I was going to phone the police when you turned up.'

'Then do it now,' he snapped. 'I bet Matt's kidnapped him. I bet he's miles away. I knew he spelled trouble the moment he turned up.'

* * *

136

Nicole frowned. She hadn't even thought about Matt. Would he have done that? Would he have taken Aaron? Her heart sank as she recalled how friendly he'd been. She'd actually liked the guy, and Aaron had liked him too. It would have been easy to coax him into his car. What had she done?

She felt devastated as she made her call. If anything happened to his grandson Ross would never forgive her. And nor would she be able to live with the knowledge that she was responsible for bringing even more heartache into his life.

The police promised to be there as soon as possible, reassuring her that small children were often thought missing when in reality they'd only strayed a few yards away from home.

She remembered Ross saying that the last time it had happened Aaron had been found curled up in Tilda's bed. She gave the house another search, but it revealed nothing, and Ross's mood was getting more foul with each passing second.

'You do realise,' he barked, 'that in the eyes of the law Aaron belongs to Matt? That I don't have a leg to stand on?'

'You don't know that Matt's taken him,' she tried to reason.

'I know,' he barked. 'Aaron would never have wandered away on his own.'

'Little boys do,' she pointed out.

'Not Aaron. He's had it instilled into him that he never goes anywhere without me or Tilda. Or you, of course.' But the look he gave her said without words that he'd never trust her with his grandson again.

She felt sick inside. What was she to do? She'd been in her seventh heaven this morning. Everything had been going well between her and Ross; she'd felt so much hope for the future. And now? It was doubtful she'd even be allowed to stay.

'You've searched the estuary, you say?'

Nicole nodded.

'I'd better take a look myself. You wait for the police. And Nicole—' he gave her a menacing look '—if he's not found safe and well then you'd better look out.'

She wanted to argue that it wasn't her fault, that he was being unfair, but she knew that he was hurting and lashing out and probably didn't mean what he said. And who was she trying to kid? Of course he meant it. He'd probably kill her if he lost Aaron altogether, and to hell with the consequences.

Two police officers came and asked for a full description and a photograph and tried to reassure her, and Ross returned from his search and told them of his fears that his grandson had been kidnapped.

'And have you grounds for this theory, Mr Dufrais?' asked one of them.

Ross shook his head. 'But I know.'

'How can you be sure?'

'He's been hanging around.'

'And he's the boy's father, you say?'

'In so much as that he made my daughter pregnant,' said Ross. 'But when he found out he didn't want to know.'

'I see. And what is his full name and where does he live?'

'It's Matthew Cooper, but I don't know his address. Nicole—did he tell you?'

'Nicole is your wife, is that right, Mr Dufrais? The boy's grandmother?' The PC looked curiously at Nicole.

'No, she's not Aaron's grandmother,' informed Ross irritably. 'We've only been married a few weeks. My first wife died, so did the boy's mother—not that that has anything to do with it.'

'Ah!' said the police officer.

'And what the hell's that supposed to mean?' asked Ross with a furious frown.

'It does throw some light on why you suspect the boy's father may have taken him. If his mother's dead, then—'

'Then nothing,' snarled Ross. 'Aaron's mine.'

'You're his legal guardian?'

'Not exactly.'

'You've adopted him?'

'Well, no, but for goodness' sake, man, I'm his grandfather. He lives with me. I love him dearly and he loves me. He wouldn't be happy with anyone else, especially not that swine Matthew Cooper. He has no claim on him whatsoever.'

'I can see how you feel, Mr Dufrais, but the fact of the matter is—'

Ross's anger broke. 'What the hell are we doing discussing Aaron's parentage when he's missing? Go out and find him, for pity's sake. The longer you leave it the further away he'll be.'

'Matt's mother lives in Bude,' Nicole said. 'He was staying with her.'

'You have the address?'

'No.'

'Never mind. We'll find her. I'm sure you're worrying unnecessarily, Mr Dufrais. Aaron will turn up safe and sound. We'll instigate a police search, of course, and also track down the boy's father. In the meantime—'

'In the meantime I'll go out of my mind,' roared Ross, and as soon as the two men had gone he turned on Nicole again. 'I'm holding you fully responsible, of course.'

'You think I'm feeling happy about it?' Nicole riposted. 'You think I turned my back on him deliberately? Lord, Ross, I'm as worried as you.'

He snorted derisively. 'Have you any idea, any idea at all, how much he means to me?'

'Of course I do.' She wanted to hold him, to put her arms around him and reassure him, but she knew that he would toss her away. Their closeness of the morning had gone, was probably irretrievably lost for evermore.

'I'm beginning to wonder.'

'Ross, please, don't do this to yourself. He's only been missing for a little over half an hour. He'll turn up safe and sound; I'm sure he will.'

'I trusted you.' There was a glint of steel in his dark eyes. 'I trusted you, Nicole. You've let me down.'

A chill struck through her heart. This was the end. Even if—no, not if—when Aaron was found, he would still blame her; he would banish her from his life. Their marriage contract would finish earlier rather than later. She would never see him again.

The next hour passed painfully slowly. Tilda was feeling too ill to get out of her bed so Nicole sat with her. She was safer away from Ross, because he did nothing but rant and rave and fling further accusations.

'Ross doesn't mean half of what he says,' said Tilda sympathetically. 'You'll see. Once Aaron's found he'll realise that he's being unfair. It was my fault, after all. I distracted you away from Aaron.'

Nicole grimaced. 'Of course it wasn't your fault. And Ross's right; I should have brought him indoors with me.'

'How were any of us to know that he'd disappear like that? He's played outside a thousand times. But I know how you're feeling. He disappeared once when I was supposed to be keeping an eye on him.'

'Do you really think that Matt's taken him?' asked Nicole. 'Or do you think he's just wandered away? He could be lying hurt somewhere. You know how he loves those rock pools. Maybe he slipped and banged his head. I think I'll go and take another look.'

The woman put a staying hand on Nicole's arm. 'I know you want to feel that you're doing something useful, but the police have taken over; they'll find him if he's there. And as for Matt—well, as I don't know him I don't know how his mind works. I was surprised to hear he'd turned up, considering he's made no contact whatsoever over the years. Was it really him you spoke to, do you reckon? Or is Ross being overly suspicious?'

Nicole shrugged. 'All I know is that he told me his name was Matt. Ross surmised the rest.'

'As he would,' said Tilda sagely. 'He's paranoid about losing the child. Which is perfectly understandable, of course. He should have done something about it when Tara died. But he was afraid of stirring up a hornets' nest.'

'Did Tara ever speak about Matt?' It was a question she'd never dared ask Ross.

'I remember when she came home pregnant.' Tilda's grey eyes were suddenly faraway. 'Poor child, she was heartbroken that Matt had ditched her. She was desperately in love with him.' And, with a wry twist of her lips, 'I guess the responsibility scared him—a lot of young men are like that.

'And, yes, over the years she did talk about him. She'd wonder where he was and what he was doing, whether he was married. Whether Aaron had any little half-brothers or sisters. I think deep down she thought Aaron ought to know who his father was, and yet at other times she'd call him all the names under the sun, declaring that if she ever saw him she'd lay into him until he wished he'd never met her.'

Nicole smiled. 'She sounds very much like her father.'

Tilda nodded. 'She undoubtedly had his temperament, though in looks she took after Alison.'

'Why are there no photos around?' This was something else that had always puzzled Nicole.

A wistful smile. 'Ross's doing, I'm afraid. He said he had enough memories in his head without having to look at them every day. It's part of his guilt, I think.'

'It seems such a pity.'

'It is,' agreed Tilda. 'But he has you now,' she added brightly. 'I've seen such a difference in him. He's back to his old self. I'd venture to say he's even happier.'

'Until I lost Aaron,' said Nicole wryly, sadly. 'Oh, Tilda, I feel truly awful. And he won't let me near him. I want to console him and yet…' She tailed off and listened. 'Did you hear something? Did you hear a voice? I think it's Aaron.' She shot to her feet and looked out of the window. And sure enough, walking up the pathway to the cottage was Aaron, hand in hand with—of all people—Matt's mother.

Nicole gaped. There was no other word for it. Mrs Cooper was laughing, Aaron was chattering, and they seemed not to have a care in the world.

'He's back,' she called over her shoulder as she raced down the stairs. 'He's safe.'

Ross was at the door before her. He wrenched it open and glared at the woman, then he took Aaron's hand and snatched him away from her. 'Who the hell are you, and what is going on?'

Mrs Cooper looked totally startled. 'I—I'm sorry—I—'

'It's Matt's mother,' said Nicole from over Ross's shoulder.

He turned to her and frowned. 'Matt's mother? How the hell do you know that?'

'Grandpa, Grandpa.' Aaron, looking faintly worried, tugged at his grandfather's sleeve. 'I've been to the café. I had ice cream and a doughnut and Nanna says she's—'

All hell broke loose.

Ross, looking as though he was about to explode, glowered down at the boy. '*What* did you call her?'

'Nanna,' he whispered, realising that he'd done something wrong but he didn't know what. 'She told me to.'

Ross turned his attention to the woman who by now was trembling violently and wringing her hands. '*Nanna?*'

Nicole could see that Mrs Cooper was so stunned by this unexpected attack that she was on the verge of collapse, and she went to her and took her arm. 'I think we should talk this over inside.'

'You're dead right we need to talk,' Ross exclaimed. 'You know this woman, Nicole? And yet you never told me you'd met her? My God, what's been going on behind my back?'

Once inside, with the door firmly closed, Ross said to Aaron, 'I think you'd better go and tell Tilda you're back.'

The boy needed no second bidding. He ran up the stairs as though his life depended on it.

'And you, Nicole,' Ross went on, 'phone the police and tell them he's turned up.'

And leave him to deal with Mrs Cooper, thought Nicole. The poor woman. She didn't want to leave her, but she knew better than to argue. It didn't take more than a couple of minutes, though, to make the call, and when she returned to the living room Mrs Cooper was seated and Ross was standing over her.

The woman was still shaking and Ross was shouting—and they were getting nowhere because Matt's mother was too shocked to speak.

'Ross.' Nicole approached him. 'Sit down. Let's talk reasonably. You'll find nothing out like that.'

Mrs Cooper gave her a weak, but grateful smile. Ross, on the other hand, blasted her with eyes as hard as flint. 'Talk reasonably when this woman walked off with my grandson?'

'How do you know she walked off with him? You've not given her a chance to speak. Maybe she found Aaron, maybe she was returning him. Have you thought of that?'

It was clear Ross hadn't, because just for a moment he looked shaken. And he finally sat. 'You'd better tell me the whole story,' he said gruffly.

'Would you like a cup of tea, Mrs Cooper?' asked Nicole. She wanted to stay and listen but the woman looked in desperate need of something to steady her nerves. 'Or a drop of brandy perhaps?'

'Yes,' she whispered. 'That would be nice. Brandy.'

Ross grunted but he got up to pour it, pushing the glass into the woman's still shaking hand.

She took a sip and closed her eyes as it slid down her throat. Nicole and Ross watched. She took another sip, and another, and finally she stopped shaking and the colour began to return to her cheeks. But not until she'd finished the drink did she say anything.

'I meant no harm to Aaron, I just wanted to talk to him.'

'You could have talked outside the cottage,' growled Ross. 'Why did you take him away?'

The woman shrugged. 'I don't know.'

'What do you mean, you don't know?' he asked harshly.

His loud voice made Mrs Cooper jump and look decidedly nervous all over again. 'I don't know,' she said again in a weak, trembling voice.

'Matt's put you up to this, hasn't he?'

Bright blue eyes started to water. 'I don't know what you mean.'

'Heaven help me!' exclaimed Ross. 'Don't you know anything, woman?'

'You're making me nervous.'

'And how the hell do you think I felt when my grandson went missing?'

'He's my grandson too,' said Mrs Cooper in a faint, apologetic voice. 'And he was perfectly safe.'

'But *I* didn't know that, did I?' asked Ross. 'I've been out of my mind with worry. And who's to know you wouldn't have brought him back if you hadn't seen the police out searching?'

'Ross!' Nicole thought he was being too hard.

'What police?' The woman's voice was faint and squeaky and full of terror. 'Are they going to lock me up?'

Ross clenched his fists and closed his eyes, holding on to his patience by a thin thread.

Nicole spoke softly to their reluctant visitor. 'We rang them when we couldn't find Aaron. They've been out looking for him. But you needn't worry. Of course you won't go to jail.' And she glared at Ross for frightening her.

'I wasn't going to keep him. I just wanted to—'

'Talk to him. Yes, we know,' cut in Ross sharply. 'Why didn't you knock on the door and ask?'

The woman shrank back into her seat. She was tiny anyway, but she seemed even smaller the way she withdrew. 'I—couldn't. You wouldn't have let me. I just wanted to see Aaron on my own, just once, just to see what my grandson was like, to speak with him. I—'

'How did you know where we lived?' interrupted Ross curtly.

'I—we—Matt knew. You see—when my husband died—' fresh tears coursed down her cheeks '—I felt so alone. There's only Matt, and although he's married he has no children. And he lives in London so I don't see him very often.'

Once started, Mrs Cooper couldn't stop. 'When he came here to rest I asked him about the girl he'd made pregnant at university. I had a grandchild somewhere whom I'd never seen. I asked him to find out where they were living.'

'So that you could kidnap him?' Ross asked icily.

'No, no!' the woman replied, her hands clutching the empty glass.

Nicole felt sorry for her. She could see both sides of the story. She could understand that fear of losing Aaron was making Ross angry, but she could also appreciate the woman's wish to see her unknown grandchild. It was a very natural thing for her to want to do.

'Like I said, I wanted to see my grandchild, just once.'

'And I'm supposed to believe that?' demanded Ross. 'I'm supposed to believe that you won't be back, that you won't hang around looking for another opportunity to take Aaron away?'

'Not without your permission.' The woman looked at him in both hope and fear.

'Which as you very well know I'm not likely to give,' he rasped. 'How did Matt find us?'

The woman continued to twist the glass in her hands, clearly still dreadfully nervous of Ross. 'He remembered Tara saying that her parents had a holiday cottage at St Meek. I think it was the fact that they both came from Cornwall that drew them together in the first place. He asked a few questions in the village, found out where the cottage was, but it was coincidence that Matt saw Aaron on the beach one day with—with this lady here.'

'My wife,' he growled, glancing coldly at Nicole.

Mrs Cooper looked startled. 'I didn't know. My son said she looked after Aaron for you.'

'So she does. But it's hardly the point. You were saying?'

'Well, that it was coincidence.'

'How did Matt know Aaron was his child?'

'I guess you know your own flesh and blood,' she answered with a faint wry smile. 'But Aaron told him that his name was Dufrais. It's not very common, is it? Matt still couldn't be sure, of course, so he kept an eye open for this lady here, saw where she lived, and knew then without a shadow of doubt that Aaron was his son. I'm sorry to hear what happened to your daughter.'

'And how the hell do you know that?'

The woman glanced apprehensively at Nicole.

Nicole lifted her chin. 'I told Matt.'

His eyes warred with hers. 'I'll speak to you later, madam,' he said firmly, and, to Mrs Cooper, 'I still don't see why you took Aaron off without telling anyone.'

'I only meant it to be for a minute. But then he asked to go to the café, and the time went by, and I—I didn't think,' she finished lamely.

'You didn't think we'd notice he was missing?' he asked, his voice loaded with sarcasm, his dark eyes still condemning.

'I was so happy to be with him. He's adorable. Such a clever little boy. Such a chatterbox. So much like Matt when—'

'He's like his mother,' insisted Ross.

'He looks like you,' said Mrs Cooper.

Faintly mollified, Ross failed to retort.

'Shall I make us some tea?' asked Nicole.

'That would be nice,' said Matt's mother.

'Thank you,' added Ross, and she felt his eyes on her as she left the room.

She could hear the murmur of their voices and was relieved to note that Ross was no longer shouting. While the kettle boiled she ran upstairs to see whether Tilda and Aaron wanted a drink, and gave Ross's aunt a brief rundown on what had happened, although Aaron had already told her his version of the story.

'All's well that ends well,' said Tilda with satisfaction.

When Nicole returned to the living room with a loaded tray Mrs Cooper and Ross were sitting in silence. She glanced at them anxiously but they seemed to have reached a truce.

Ross no longer glowered at the woman, and she no longer looked scared to death of him. But there was still a sense of uneasiness as they drank their tea, and as soon as she had finished Mrs Cooper announced that she was leaving.

'I'm sorry for the trouble I've caused,' she said. 'I didn't mean it.'

Nicole expected Ross to jump down her throat again, but he didn't, he murmured something that sounded suspiciously like, 'You can come and see him again.'

But of course when the woman was gone he turned on Nicole. 'You never told me you'd met that woman.'

She grimaced. 'I knew you'd be angry. It was something I couldn't avoid.'

'You're damn right I'm angry. I could have lost Aaron through your foolishness. You let your tongue run away with you, madam. Don't you realise that there're times when it's best to say nothing?'

'You're speaking with hindsight.'

'I'm speaking the truth. If your thoughtlessness had—'

'I know,' Nicole cut in fiercely. 'You'd have banished me from your life. Maybe I should go anyway. I don't seem to have brought you any happiness.'

Their eyes met and held. Nicole felt a frisson of awareness run through her, a memory of last night and the sheer breathtaking quality of their lovemaking. She had felt so close to him then; now a chasm a mile wide stood between them, one it was doubtful they'd ever be able to bridge.

'No,' he said at length. 'I don't want you to go. Aaron's just getting used to you and I don't want Tilda disappointed.'

So that was it. It wasn't himself he was thinking about, but Aaron and Tilda. He could do without her quite easily.

Those nights of passion meant nothing.

Nicole swallowed her hurt and watched him as he strode from the room. Their love affair had been short and sweet.

Ross knew that he was being unnecessarily hard on Nicole, but, dammit, she'd nearly lost him his grandson. His biggest nightmare had almost come true.

Did Matt want Aaron? Had he put his mother up to it? Was it the beginning of a series of incidents that would end with Aaron disappearing altogether?

He couldn't go on like this; he had to make sure Aaron was legally his and that Matt could never take him away. He must call his solicitor. Meantime Aaron had to be told that what he'd done was wrong.

Tilda looked at him steadily as he entered her room. 'She's gone?'

'Yes,' he replied tersely.

'I heard you shouting.'

'She deserved it.'

'Poor woman.'

'Poor woman?' he scorned. 'How can you take her side?'

'I know what she did was wrong,' his aunt answered mildly, 'but she didn't harm Aaron. It seems to me that he had a good time.'

Ross looked down at his grandson, curled up on Tilda's bed, his hand tucked tightly into hers. He looked afraid of him, and that was a shock because Aaron adored his grandfather as a rule.

'Come here, Aaron.'

The boy looked anxiously at Tilda, who smiled and nodded, and very slowly he stood up on the bed. But instead of bouncing into Ross's arms the way he usually did he edged his way nervously towards him, his eyes downcast, his little hands clenched together.

Ross picked him up and held him close to his chest. His beloved grandson. All that was left of his family. 'Aaron, Aaron,' he muttered into his hair, 'don't ever do that to me again.'

Then he held him at arm's length and looked into his face. 'It's wrong, Aaron, to go off with someone without asking permission. I thought you knew that.'

'I like the lady.'

'Maybe you do, but she's a stranger. I've always told you never to talk to strangers.'

Aaron frowned. 'Not a stranger. I saw her before. In the café. With the money man.'

'The money man?'

'I think he means Matt,' said Tilda.

So Nicole had had a cosy meeting with Matt and his mother and very conveniently kept it from him. She had a lot of explaining to do. 'You didn't tell me, Aaron.' He was finding it extremely difficult to keep his voice calm.

'I forgot. I won't do it again, Grandpa. Are you still cross with me?'

Ross hugged the boy close to him again. 'Of course not. I wasn't angry with you; I was worried because you'd gone missing.'

'You shouted.'

'I'm sorry.'

Aaron wrapped his arms round his grandfather's neck. 'I love you, Grandpa.'

'And I love you, more than you'll ever know.' The tension was slowly easing out of him but it would be a long time before he forgave Nicole. He'd entrusted her with his precious grandson and she'd jeopardised his safety. That was something he would never forget.

CHAPTER ELEVEN

To SAY Nicole was surprised when she opened the door and saw Matt Cooper was putting it mildly. Her mouth fell open. 'You! What are you doing here? If Ross catches you he'll—'

'Is Mr Dufrais in?'

'Well, yes, but—'

'I'd like a word with him.'

A few days had gone by since Aaron went missing—a few days in which Ross had hardly said a word to her, except to chastise her over and over again for putting his grandson in danger. He'd accused her of colluding with the Coopers, had not listened when she'd tried to explain that each meeting had been accidental, and as for them sleeping together—it didn't happen. He banished her to her old bedroom and didn't seem to care what Tilda thought.

Except that his aunt didn't know, because she wasn't well enough to leave her bed.

'I doubt he'll want to speak to you,' she told Matt.

'There are things I need to clear up.'

Nicole nodded. 'Very well, I'll tell him you're here. I daren't ask you in until—'

'That's OK. I understand.'

'Is your mother all right?' she asked tentatively, wondering whether his visit had something to do with his mother's health. Ross really had laid in to her. What if she'd suffered a heart attack or something equally serious?

Matt smiled wryly. 'She's fine.'

'Good. Well—I'll go and get him.'

It seemed very rude, leaving him standing on the doorstep, but she knew how Ross would react if she invited Matt in. She didn't want to be the cause of all hell breaking loose yet again.

Ross was shut away in his den doing some paperwork. He'd not left the house since Aaron's adventure unless he took his grandson with him, telling Nicole without the need for words that he no longer trusted her. She was beginning to wonder why he'd insisted that she stay.

She tapped uneasily on his door.

'Come in.'

He looked tired, she thought, as though the weight of the world sat on his shoulders, almost back to what he'd been like the first time she saw him. He even had on the same red sweater.

Nicole hadn't realised how much better he'd been looking until she saw him like this. And it was all her fault! 'You have a visitor,' she said in a flat voice.

His eyes were cold, shutting her out, excluding her from his life.

She wished that she could do the same, but it was impossible. She loved this man despite everything. Loved him so much that her stomach flipped just looking at him, her pulses felt as though they were being driven by an electric motor, and her heart threatened to burst out of her chest.

'Who is it?' he demanded curtly.

Taking a steadying breath, and curling her fingers into fists behind her back, Nicole answered, 'Matt Cooper.' And waited for the explosion.

It wasn't long in coming. 'What the devil is he doing here?' And he jumped to his feet. 'I hope you told him to get lost?' Then, 'No, I'll see him; I need to see him. I know why he's here. But he needn't think that.' He tailed off. 'Where is he?'

Nicole moved out of his way as he headed towards the door. 'He's outside. I—'

But Ross had already gone.

Ross hadn't expected things to move this quickly. His solicitor had said that there were lengthy procedures to go through—and yet Matt was here, now, and for what other reason than to tell him he had a fight on his hands?

The front door was open. Matt stood on the cobbled path, his hands shoved into trouser pockets, his back towards Ross. There was nothing aggressive about his stance; he didn't look as though he'd come to pick a fight. But Ross wasn't fooled.

'Yes?' He spoke loudly and crossly. 'What do you want?'

'Ah, Mr Dufrais.' Matt smiled as he turned and held out his hand.

Ross ignored it.

'I've come to apologise for my mother's behaviour.'

'Apologise?' This threw Ross; it wasn't what he'd expected.

'Yes. She had no right taking Aaron like that.'

'You're damn right she hadn't. She's lucky I'm not pressing charges.'

Matt heaved a sigh. 'Thank you for that. I've only just found out, you see. I was back home in London when it happened. She phoned and told me. I caught the first train. It's appalling, and she really is very sorry.'

Ross rubbed the tips of his fingers across his brow. This man had caught him unawares.

'You see,' went on Matt, 'since my father's death she hasn't been herself. She's lonely as hell and I'm sure she wasn't thinking straight when she took Aaron.'

'I think maybe you'd better come in,' invited Ross. He appreciated Matt's visit on his mother's behalf, and it helped to hear that her intentions hadn't been serious, but he wasn't finished with him. There were other things to be sorted, other promises to be extracted. 'Would you like a beer?'

Matt looked surprised. 'Please.'

They went into the kitchen where Ross reached two cans out of the fridge, passed one to Matt and kept one himself, pulling the ring and taking a swig out of the can. It was something he didn't normally do—he'd rather drink out of a glass, and in fact he preferred whisky—but this was an unusual situation. He motioned Matt to sit down.

'Nicole told me your mother asked you to see if you could trace—er—Aaron.' He couldn't bring himself to say, your son, because as far as he was concerned Matt was no father of Aaron's. Never had been, never would be.

'That's right. She feels she's been done out of a grand-child.'

Ross's lips clamped. 'I hope you're not getting any ideas of—'

'No, sir,' interrupted Matt at once. 'I gave up my rights to Tara's child the day I walked out. I'm well aware of that. But it doesn't mean to say that I haven't thought about Tara and my son, whether she was well, whether they were both well. I have, frequently, and I'm thoroughly ashamed of what I did.'

'As you should be,' said Ross sternly. 'But for the record, in case you change your mind, I think you should know that I intend to formally adopt Aaron. I trust you'll raise no objections?'

A wave of sadness crossed Matt's face but he squared his shoulders and shook his head. 'No, I won't. As a matter of fact I've just cheered my mother up and I'd like to share the good news with you.'

Ross frowned, wondering why it should concern him.

'My wife's finally pregnant. My mother's going to have a grandchild, after all—two of them, actually. Yvonne's expecting twins.'

'Congratulations.' Ross didn't actually smile, but he shook the man's hand. 'Does your wife know about Aaron?'

'She does now,' Matt admitted. 'I had to tell her what Mother had done.'

'And she's OK about it?'

'Yes.' He inclined his head a trifle sadly. 'You'll have no trouble from us.'

Ross actually began to feel guilty now that Matt was being so reasonable. Maybe he'd done him an injustice all these years. 'Um, er, maybe you and your mother can see Aaron occasionally.'

Matt beamed his pleasure then. 'I'd like that.'

'Though I don't plan to tell him that you're his father. At least not yet. Perhaps when he's older.'

'I understand. And, sir, I'm very sorry about Tara. I did love her; I truly did.' Tears came to Matt's eyes as he spoke. 'I was just so scared at the time. I've been regretting it ever since.'

Ross nodded slowly. 'One thing we can't do is put back the clock. I might not have Tara but I have Aaron; he means the world to me. And you're going to have your own family soon. Cherish your children. They'll bring you more pleasure than you can ever dream of. Heartache too, I guess, but one makes up for the other.'

After Matt had left Ross returned to the kitchen and sat for a while thinking over their conversation. He didn't hear Nicole enter, he didn't even see her because he had his back to the door, but her fragrance gave her away. It filled his nostrils and more than anything he wanted to turn and take her into his arms.

He was annoyed with her, he was as angry as hell, but he still couldn't dismiss her from his life. She still tormented him, still turned his insides to mush, and life without her would be unbearable.

'Are you all right, Ross?' She spoke in a whisper, as though afraid he might lash out at her as he had done on so many occasions since Aaron's disappearance.

'Yes.'

'What did Matt want?'

He turned then and looked at her, saw the beautiful girl he'd fallen in love with—because he'd finally, reluctantly, accepted that he *was* in love with her—her gorgeous blue eyes troubled, her face pale and full of concern. 'To apologise.'

A faint frown tugged her brows. 'For what?'

'His mother's behaviour.'

'I see.'

He wondered if she really did when the whole affair had been her fault. If she'd kept her mouth shut, if she hadn't told them who Aaron was— Although apparently Aaron had piped up with his own name. Maybe he shouldn't lay all the blame on her.

'And to say that he has no intention of taking Aaron from me.'

She managed a smile then. 'That's good.'

'*If* he keeps his word.'

'Did he give you any reason to believe that he wouldn't?'

'No,' Ross admitted. 'But I've learned never to trust anyone completely.'

He could tell by her crushed expression that she thought he meant her too. And he did. But perhaps it was time to relent. 'I've been thinking,' he said. 'I've decided to move back to Exeter, after all.'

'I see.'

That was all she said. He couldn't tell whether she was pleased or not. 'Aaron will be safer there.'

'But I thought you said that Matt—'

'I did, but his mother might feel the urge again. I can't afford to take the risk. I'll tell Tilda. We'll begin packing straight away. I intended returning before Christmas anyway.'

'Do you think Tilda's up to it?' she asked with a frown.

He appreciated her concern; it was one of the things he loved about her. She cared for Tilda and Aaron as though they were her own. He really ought not to have been so hard on her. It was fear that did it, of course. Fear that his life was going to be turned upside down again, that he was going to lose those he loved most.

What were Nicole's feelings for him? he wondered. Physically they were in complete tune with each other. But did she love him? Or did she hate him? Had he treated her so abominably that when her contract ended she would be glad to escape?

He shook the thought from his mind. 'I'll check with the doctor, of course,' he told her, 'but in actual fact she'll be better off because it's nearer the hospital.'

'So what do you want me to do?'

Come to bed with me. He dismissed the thought the instant it was born. It was craziness. 'You could make a start with Aaron's toys. I've no doubt he'll love to help. You can maybe turn it into an adventure?'

'So that he doesn't get stroppy about moving, you mean?'

It was quiet censure, and he knew he deserved it, but he nodded nevertheless. 'Something like that.'

'And when you're settled in your other home will my contract be finished?'

Alarm rose in him. What was she saying? That she wanted out? 'Of course not, Nicole,' he said quietly. 'I still need you.' But he couldn't bring himself to take her into his arms and give her the reassurance he knew she deserved. Something still held him back. Something locked deep within him.

*   *   *

It was hardly the encouragement she needed, thought Nicole sadly as she turned and left the kitchen. In fact Ross couldn't have made it any plainer that the sensual side of their relationship, the side that had sent her soaring with the stars, was over. She was back to doing the job he paid her for.

Maybe if Tilda had been mobile he might have made more of an effort, but since his aunt had no idea what their sleeping arrangements were it didn't seem to worry him. Obviously his feelings for her had never run deep.

Perhaps it was for the best, she decided, trying to rationalise her own feelings. There was no doubt that she'd been afraid her heart might break at the end of her contract.

This way, the finish of their affair had come sooner rather than later. She would put on a brave face, she'd throw herself into organising their move, and once they were settled she'd have got used to the idea. Or at least that was what she told herself.

It took a week to pack everything—in between caring for Tilda and keeping Aaron from being bored. He didn't like the idea of moving. He couldn't remember the old house and he threw tantrum after tantrum.

'I don't want to go,' he repeated. 'I want to stay here.'

'But there's more room,' Nicole told him. 'You'll have lots more space to play, and a huge garden, and there's probably other little boys you can make friends with.'

'Don't want no one,' he retorted, stamping his feet.

'It's where Grandpa and Tilda used to live. They're looking forward to going back.'

'And Mummy? Did she live there when she was a little girl?'

Nicole nodded. It was the first time Aaron had asked about his mother. She knew Ross mentioned Tara frequently, but the boy had said nothing to her. 'I bet Grandpa will let you sleep in her old room. Won't that be nice?'

Aaron thought about it. 'Mummy's gone to heaven.'

'Yes, I know, darling.'

'Won't she ever come back?'

'I'm afraid not.'

'I want another mummy.'

'You have me,' she whispered, going down on her knees and hugging him to her. 'I love you heaps.'

'I love you too, Nicole. Tell me about the big house.'

'It's like a prince's palace,' came Ross's voice from behind. 'There are lots of rooms for little boys to play and hide.'

'Grandpa!' Aaron ran into Ross's arms.

Nicole wondered how long he'd been standing there, whether he approved of her telling Aaron how much she loved him because of the implications when she left? On the other hand what was she expected to say? The poor little boy was craving the love of a mother figure.

But Ross said nothing. He stayed and told Aaron all about the house. 'It has twelve rooms,' he said. 'You can have a bedroom as well as a playroom, and when you make friends you can have them to sleep over.'

Aaron's eyes opened wide. '*Grandpa!* When are we going?'

'Tomorrow.'

Aaron jumped up and down for joy. 'We're going tomorrow. We're going tomorrow,' he sang. 'Nicole, we're going tomorrow.'

'I think that's settled, then,' said Ross. 'Nicole, when you've got a minute I'd like a word with you.'

Uh-oh, she thought, this is it. But it wasn't to tell her off, it was to explain that he'd arranged an ambulance for Tilda. 'And I'd like you to go with her,' he added. 'We'll do it before Aaron gets up. I don't want him to see how poorly she really is. Court House is ready to accept her. I have staff there who're fully acquainted with the situation.

She ought to be in hospital, of course, but she flatly refuses. She wants to return to Court House. She loves that place. I've arranged for a full-time nurse.'

Was he saying that Tilda was going home to die? wondered Nicole. Heavens. It didn't bear thinking about. She'd come to love Tilda as if she were her own flesh and blood. In fact she loved the whole Dufrais family, and it would be the biggest wrench of her life when the time came for her to leave.

She wondered if Ross had thought what it would do to Aaron. The boy would not only lose his beloved Tilda, but Nicole as well. He'd be left alone with his grandpa in a house large enough to accommodate an army—and when Ross was out at work what then? A live-in nanny? Another strange woman? Someone else for Aaron to get used to?

'You look deep in thought.'

'I was wondering what was going to happen to Aaron.'

Ross frowned. 'What do you mean? He's going to love it at Court House. Tara used to have a ball, running in and out of all of the rooms. And there's almost three acres of garden. It's made for children.'

Nicole came straight to the point. 'I wasn't thinking of the immediate future. But when Tilda's—gone, I'll have served my purpose. Aaron will have no one except you.'

'We'll talk about that when the time comes,' said Ross bluntly.

Nicole had half expected—no, hoped—that he'd say there was no need for her to go. It had been a foolish wish. She might as well accept the fact that when the time came he'd shake her hand, he'd say, Goodbye, thank you very much, and then he would never think of her again.

Well—maybe he'd think of her, but only as someone who'd helped him out in his hour of need. He wouldn't be heartbroken because he'd never given her his heart. He'd enjoyed a few weeks of lust, and that was all. Even that hadn't lasted very long.

Court House was a splendid L-shaped redbrick house on the outskirts of Exeter, set well back from the road. Not quite like a palace, although Nicole was sure Aaron would be satisfied.

It had been built to Ross's specification: the rooms spacious and airy, and the gardens not in the least formal. Perfect for little boys to play in.

The first thing that Nicole noticed after she'd got Tilda settled and was waiting for Ross and Aaron to arrive were the many photos of Alison and Tara all over the place. Pictures of Ross too, family groups, single portraits, informal holiday shots.

This was more homely than the cottage, she decided. Despite the size of the house it was decorated warmly and compassionately, and there were lots of ornaments and pictures that were obviously holiday souvenirs which had all found a home here.

She was still looking at the photos when Ross came in. 'Put them away if you like,' he told her, tight-lipped. 'Anything you don't like just change. I shan't mind.'

But Nicole shook her head. 'I don't think so. The photos don't worry me. In any case they're good for Aaron. He must never forget his mother and his grandma. Tara was beautiful, wasn't she?'

He nodded proudly. 'The best. You really like children, don't you?'

'Yes, I do. I love going to my sister's and playing with her children. I'm godmother to two of them.' Though unforgivably she hadn't been to see them since getting married to Ross.

'Do you plan to have any of your own?'

'If I ever meet a man who loves me enough,' she answered.

'You'll be free soon.'

It wasn't what Nicole wanted to hear and she felt a rush of tears. As she wasn't a tearful person it surprised her. Good Lord, she'd known from the beginning what the rules of the game were, so why get weepy now?

But she knew why. She loved Ross and she wanted him to love her. If only it was something she could order to happen. She heaved a sigh. 'Which is my room?'

Each room had an *en suite* bathroom, and Ross had put Nicole next to him, though she noticed it had an adjoining door. And when she opened the wardrobe to hang up her clothes she realised why. It was full of Alison's clothes—his wife must have used it as a dressing room, and he'd either forgotten or couldn't bring himself to get rid of them.

She tapped on the adjoining door and heard Ross draw back the bolt. 'I'm sorry to trouble you,' she said, 'but I seem to have a problem.'

Ross frowned, and then his eyes slid past her to the open wardrobe doors. 'Oh, hell. I'm sorry, I'd forgotten.'

And she could see that he was truly shaken. Obviously he'd been too traumatised after the accident to get rid of them and now he was embarrassed.

'Shall I bag them and send them to a charity shop?' she asked quickly.

He looked relieved by her suggestion. 'Would that be too much for you?'

'Of course not.'

'I'm so sorry. I should have had them cleared out. I—'

'It's all right,' insisted Nicole. 'I understand. Is there anything you want to keep?'

'No. Get rid of the lot,' he said with quiet determination, then he closed the door quickly again.

And so Nicole went downstairs and Sarah the housekeeper found her some black bin liners after she'd explained what she wanted to do. 'I could do it for you, madam, if you wish? I'm new here, you see. I didn't realise that they weren't your clothes.'

But Nicole shook her head. 'No, I'll do it. And it's Nicole.' Being called madam made her sound like something she wasn't.

Nicole admired Alison's taste as she emptied hanger after hanger. They were the sort of clothes she would have worn herself—and for a brief second she wondered whether Ross had been attracted to her because she reminded him in some oblique way of his wife. She dismissed the thought as unworthy, and at last all wardrobes and drawers were empty and she was able to hang away her own clothes which, she noticed with a wry smile, took up much less space. Alison had obviously loved clothes. There were some that looked as though they'd hardly been worn.

That night Nicole found it difficult to get to sleep. She tossed and turned, trying to tell herself it was the strange bed and all that, but deep within her she knew it was because Ross was a few feet away on the other side of the door.

She had accepted the fact that he was never going to make love to her again, but that didn't stop her dreaming, or reliving those magic moments. She could almost imagine him in bed beside her, touching, arousing, exciting.

Her heart began a pagan rhythm, a drumbeat stirring her senses. Her breathing grew shallow and rapid, and deep within her she cried out for fulfilment. And then she heard another cry, a different cry—Aaron!

Sleeping in a strange house was clearly unsettling for him too, she decided as she leapt out of bed and pulled on her dressing gown.

She and Ross both emerged from their doors at the same time. He wore a pair of burgundy boxer shorts and was in the act of shrugging into a navy and burgundy striped towelling robe.

For just a moment Nicole couldn't take her eyes off him. She wanted to touch that olive-skinned chest with its swirling dark hair; she wanted to run her palms over the flatness of his stomach, dip inside those shorts, stir something in him so that… God, was she crazy? He didn't want her, he'd finished with her, he'd satisfied his desire, why couldn't she get that into her thick head?

The fact that he was looking at her too with a similar kind of hunger escaped her, and when Aaron called out again they both snapped to their senses.

'I'll go,' said Ross. 'There's no point in both of us losing sleep.'

'I couldn't sleep anyway,' she told him frankly. 'I'll come with you.'

He gave her a look which suggested it was a bad idea but she took no notice. She was as concerned for Aaron as Ross, and besides she wanted to be near him. It was better than nothing at all, better than lying in her bed fancying him something rotten and being unable to do anything about it.

So she followed. By now he'd pulled on his robe, so all she could see was bare legs and bare feet. It was enough, though. Well-muscled, slightly hairy, darkly tanned like the rest of his body.

As she hurried after him her need to touch grew. She watched Ross instead of where she was going and when he paused at Aaron's door she almost cannoned into him. But then he pushed it open and went inside.

The light from the landing lit the room sufficiently to see that Aaron wasn't awake. He was dreaming, thrashing his arms, his face distorted, telling someone to leave him alone.

Ross sat on the edge of the bed and lifted Aaron into his arms. His grandson woke with a start, began to struggle, and then, realising who it was, snuggled against his chest. 'A nasty man was trying to take me away, Grandpa. You won't let him, will you?' And he looked fearfully around the room.

'It was a dream, my darling, a bad dream. There's no man here. No one's going to take you away from me, not ever.'

Then Aaron saw Nicole, and he put an arm out to her too.

So she perched on the bed as well and hugged Aaron, her body pressed against Ross's as she did so, arms and hands touching. They were like a real family, she thought, as her heart rained hammer blows against her ribcage.

Finally Aaron settled, and they put him back into bed and he fell asleep almost immediately.

Ross rubbed a hand through his hair. 'I don't know about you, but I could do with a drink,' he said as they left his grandson's room.

Nicole nodded. 'Me too. Shall I make it? What shall we have? Drinking chocolate?'

'Actually I was thinking of something stronger.'

She frowned and retorted, 'It won't help you sleep. You'll drop off, but you won't get a good night's rest.'

'Is that right, Doctor?' he asked with a wry smile. 'OK, you win. Drinking chocolate it is.'

The kitchen at Court House was nothing like the cosy room at the cottage. It was massive and modern, and filled with white cupboards and stainless steel accessories. But as a concession to its plainness the walls were colour-washed in terracotta with a stencilled pattern of birds and ivy in dark green. The ceiling was summer-blue, and the window blinds a mixture of all three colours. Consequently it wasn't as stark as it might have been.

Nicole poured milk into a jug and put it in the micro-wave. She spooned chocolate powder into mugs and mixed it with a little cold milk. And all the time Ross stood and watched her, and shivers crept down her spine, nerves tingling. Had it been a good idea coming down here together? she wondered, knowing that she would feel even less like sleep when she went back to bed.

'Are you happy, Nicole?'

It was such an unexpected question that she spun round to face him. 'Why do you ask?' She hoped he hadn't guessed at her torment.

'I've uprooted you without even enquiring how you felt about it,' he told her. 'I was guilty of having only Aaron's interests at heart.'

'I have no complaints,' she told him. 'It's not as though we're at the ends of the earth. How long does it take from St Meek to here—an hour and a quarter? It's less than sixty miles. It's nothing; I don't mind. I can still go and see my friends when I have time off.'

She wished he wouldn't look as though he was really concerned. 'In any case,' she added, trying to throw him off track, 'I'm getting paid for the job so why should I worry?'

It did the trick. With a swift frown, he demanded aggressively, 'Is that all you care about?'

Nicole shrugged. 'A girl has to earn a living,' she retorted nonchalantly. 'But you're right, I haven't been my usual self. I've been worried about Aaron. Everything that happened was my fault. And I guess his nightmare tonight was connected with it.'

The microwave pinged and she turned with relief to reach out the jug, and then almost spilt the milk when Ross came up close behind and with a groan snaked his arms around her waist. 'It wasn't your fault. I know I said it was; I know I was mad at you and I've treated you badly. I just wasn't prepared when Matt put in an appearance.'

His apology surprised her. 'But all's turned out well, surely?' she asked.

'Except for my treatment of you.' He turned her to him

and stroked her face with a trembling finger. 'Can you ever forgive me, Nicole?'

Her lovely eyes widened. 'Forgive you? It's me who should be begging forgiveness.'

'Oh, no,' he assured her strongly. 'A thousand times no. You've always done your best for Aaron. You've looked after him as though he's your own. I'm the paranoiac.'

She tried to contain a smile. The humbling of Ross Dufrais. And she shook her head. 'Maybe a little bit, but it's understandable. I know how much he means to you.'

'I wonder if you do,' he said quietly, more to himself than to her. Then he stroked a thumb across her lower lip, looking at her with hunger on his face that she hadn't seen for a long time.

A surge of hope rose within her, followed swiftly by tingling senses and quickened heartbeats. Her breathing changed, she tipped up her head to look at him and subconsciously the tip of her tongue reached out to taste his thumb, accepting, inviting, suggesting...

'Oh, Nicole.' His breath was dragged out on a groan. He lowered his head to drop featherlight kisses on her eyelids, on her nose, on her lips, his palms each side of her face, his eyes devouring.

'Do you want this as much as me?' he asked as his mouth closed on hers, his tongue searching and tormenting, tangling with hers, hinting at unbidden pleasure.

'Yes,' she whispered.

The kiss that followed was endless, and left them both panting for breath.

'Hell, I've fought against this,' Ross groaned, as he cradled her against him, stroking her damp hair from her face. 'I've told myself it's not fair on you, nor even on myself, but I can't fight it any longer.'

CHAPTER TWELVE

FALLING in love with Nicole was something that Ross hadn't wanted to do. He'd desired her, yes—what man wouldn't? She was a stunningly attractive woman. But he'd had no intention of falling in love. It was a risk he didn't dare take. Not only for his own sake but for Nicole's too. He would be putting her life in danger if he offered her any commitment.

But the truth of the matter was that he couldn't live without her. He'd finally realised how much she meant to him, and he wanted her to fall in love with him too.

It would be a miracle if it did happen. He'd made so very sure that she understood it was only a temporary marriage, even insisting she sign a piece of paper to that effect. And after the way he'd treated her she must hate the sight of him. She had every reason to walk out the second the contract came to an end.

Except that she was kissing him back—she was showing him that she did feel something for him. Maybe... Just maybe...

'Forget the chocolate,' he said gruffly, 'let's go to bed.'

But to his dismay Nicole shook her head, pushing her hands against his chest. 'I don't think that's a very good idea.'

'Why not?' Stupid question. He knew why. He'd scared her off by declaring that he could fight his feelings no longer. 'You're still mad at me?'

'I'm not mad,' she said.

'Then what?'

Nicole shook her head. 'I have my reasons.'

'But you're not sharing them with me?'

'No.' A further definite shake.

Taking advantage of the fact that she'd closed her eyes, Ross put a hand each side of her on the counter-top, effectively making her his prisoner, and then he claimed her mouth once again.

Her lovely eyes snapped open and she gave a tiny cry of protest, but he gave her no mercy. 'I don't know why you won't go to bed with me,' he muttered against her mouth, 'but I do know that you want this as much as me.'

He deepened the kiss, giving her no chance to reply, his arms urging her against him now, wanting her to feel the racing thuds of his heart.

'Oh, Nicole,' he breathed. 'What you do to me.'

'And you to me,' she seemed to say, but he couldn't be sure for she had spoken so quietly.

'You've brought me back to life again, do you know that? You've made me feel like a new man.' He kissed her impatiently, needing and demanding, desperate to break through her defences. She'd not raised them before, so why now?

Maybe she'd hoped that they'd share a bedroom once again. Maybe she was peeved that he'd put her in a separate room and was getting her own back?

Or maybe—his heart skipped a couple of beats at this point—maybe she *had* begun to fall in love with him? But because she didn't want to end up getting hurt she was attempting to shut him out.

He liked this scenario best of all. This he could work on. His kisses became more gentle, more persuasive. He ran a hand down her spine, cradled the back of her head, gentle all the time, gentle, gentle... And his patience was rewarded.

He heard the soft moan deep in her throat, he felt the tremor that ran through her, and suddenly she was kissing him with a hunger which matched his own. There was no stopping them then, and when he lifted her into his arms and carried her upstairs all she did was continue to kiss him.

Their robes came off with indecent haste, her nightie, his shorts, and after that time lost all meaning. Bodies entwined and joined, exploded, relaxed and rested, before the love-making started all over again.

He didn't dare make her any promises. Despite the fact that he was deeply in love with her he still wasn't sure that making their marriage permanent would be a good idea. What if fate stepped in again? What if something happened to her? What if she died too? It would be on his conscience for the rest of his life. He would feel even worse than he had after he'd lost his wife and daughter.

It was a sobering thought and he rolled away from her.

'Goodnight, Ross,' she said softly.

'Goodnight, Nicole.' He was glad that she'd assumed he was tired, that she had no idea of the torment in his soul.

Nicole was still sound asleep when he woke and slid silently out of bed. He had an early appointment with a catering equipment company and needed to leave at seven-thirty.

He showered, brushed his hair and shrugged into trousers and shirt. And still she slept. She looked young and inno-cent and very, very beautiful. Her cheeks were flushed, a faint smile curved her lips as though she was having a happy dream, and he longed to climb in beside her and make love all over again. But he knew that he hadn't time, so he swiftly knotted his tie, picked up his jacket, and qui-etly closed the door behind him.

His meeting had been successful, he'd placed an order at extremely competitive prices, and he was still on a high when he walked into the office he shared with Mark. But one look at his partner's serious face and he frowned. 'What's wrong?'

'Nothing.'

'Have you had a row with Marie? Is the wedding off?'

'No.'

'Trouble at one of the restaurants?'

'No.'

'Then what? You look as though the world's going to cave in on your shoulders.' A bit of an exaggeration, but his good friend did look bothered over something.

But instead of answering Mark asked a question of his own. 'How are you and Nicole getting on? I know you had a bit of a problem when Matt turned up. Have you sorted yourselves out?'

'Have we? What a question to ask. I'll tell you something, Mark, I think I'm falling in love with her. I want to turn our marriage into a proper one.' He had no compunction now about confessing his feelings to Mark. 'I guess I have a lot to thank you for. If you hadn't put that ad in we'd never have met, and—'

'I wish I hadn't.'

Ross stopped mid-flow and stared at the other man. 'Why?'

'Because—and I hate to tell you this, Ross—Nicole's not the girl you think she is. She's using you. She's simply out for all she can get.'

When Nicole awoke she was alone. She stretched and smiled and remembered last night. She'd been so determined to keep her distance from Ross, to punish him for punishing her, and yet in the end she'd been as weak as a kitten.

What a magnificent night it had been. Making love with Ross got better and better. She'd gone a little wild, she knew, but he'd seemed to like that. She wasn't in the least shy about taking the initiative, and Ross had played along with everything.

She felt sure now that he was close to falling in love with her. How could he behave like this and not be? Or was it still pure lust? Was her body all he wanted? Would he reject her as soon as she'd served her purpose?

No! She refused to think that. He was falling in love with her. He was! *He was!* And with this thought in mind she jumped out of bed, showered and dressed, and went in search of Aaron.

But when Ross came home all the pleasure of the morning had gone from his face. His dark eyes were hard and condemning, his mouth grim. 'I want a word with you,' he told her curtly. 'Come into my study.'

Nicole couldn't imagine what had happened to make him like this, what he thought she'd done—again. But there were other things that needed his attention first. 'Aaron's waiting for you to take him to bed,' she said firmly. 'He's already bathed and in his pyjamas. He's with Tilda.'

'Very well,' Ross's tone was distant, no softening of his features. 'But I shan't be long.'

Nor was he. Nicole hardly had time to puzzle over what was bothering him before he was back. Poor Aaron, she thought, he's not had much of a cuddle from his grandfather tonight, and certainly not a bedtime story.

Ross's study was an attractive book-lined room with a reproduction leather-covered desk and leather armchairs. He closed the door behind him and stood facing her. 'Tell me exactly why you agreed to marry me?'

The unexpectedness of his question sent her eyebrows shooting up. 'What are you talking about?'

'Just answer me.'

She didn't know what to say. She didn't know what he was getting at. 'What do you mean, why did I agree? You advertised; I applied. You offered; I accepted. It's as simple as that.'

'I don't think it's very simple at all,' Ross said abruptly, crossing to his desk and sitting down, indicating that she do the same.

Ross's strange behaviour was beginning to worry Nicole. He had some bee in his bonnet but she didn't know what.

'Let's talk about your job first of all,' he went on. 'The job that you quit because of harassment. You never did tell me exactly what it was that you did.'

And in that instant Nicole knew. Marie had said something to Mark. Mark had told Ross. And he'd believed every word. 'I gather you know now that I was—am—a journalist?'

'So why didn't you tell me?'

'What difference would it have made?'

'None, in the normal order of things, but we both know, don't we, that you had some ulterior motive in agreeing to marry me?'

'No, I didn't,' Nicole said firmly, adding, when he looked at her disbelievingly, 'I did when I came for the interview, I admit that, but I soon changed my mind.'

'And I'm expected to believe you?'

'It's the truth.'

'So why does Marie still think that you're going to write a story about me?'

Nicole pulled a wry face. 'I knew it was Marie,' she said, more to herself than to Ross. 'I guess I never told her that I wasn't going to do it. You must believe me, Ross.'

'Why should I?' he asked coldly. 'I bet you were all laughing at me behind my back when you applied.'

'We were intrigued,' she admitted softly, willing him to understand. 'At least I was.'

'And the others?'

'They thought there must be something wrong with you.'

Their eyes met and held, but there was nothing but coldness and reproach in his. 'Was it a dare?' he wanted to know.

'Of course not,' she answered calmly, wondering how she was going to salvage the situation when it was clear he was not going to believe her whatever she said. 'It was my own idea. I thought you must have a huge problem if you had to advertise for a wife.'

'And you were going to turn that problem to your advantage? Make money out of me, make a laughing stock out of me?'

Nicole looked down at her hands held tightly in her lap. 'Initially,' she whispered, 'I was going to write an article. But I didn't think that for long, not once I'd met you, truly I didn't.'

'Dammit, Nicole,' he growled, 'if it wasn't for Tilda I'd boot you out of the house. But let you and me get one thing very clear. As soon as my aunt—' he stopped and swallowed, finding it difficult to say his next words '—leaves this earth, you're out of here. I'll want nothing more to do with you.'

Was he overreacting? wondered Ross. Was he being too hard on Nicole? He couldn't believe how she'd tricked him. He'd thought she'd taken the job out of the kindness of her heart, that she'd felt compassion for him and for Tilda, and that she'd adored young Aaron.

How wrong he'd been, and thank goodness he'd found out in time.

It hurt like hell. Why couldn't he have discovered what she was up to before he fell in love with her? Before he'd finally convinced himself that making their marriage permanent might not be a bad thing? It went to prove that he'd been insane to even entertain such a notion.

'I thought that was the idea all along?'

Nicole's words stopped his thoughts abruptly.

'What?'

'That I leave?'

Of course. She didn't know that he'd changed his mind. Nor did she look as hurt as he felt! Damn. He'd been taking too much for granted. She enjoyed making love with him, but that was all. It wouldn't bother her in the least when her job was finished. She'd made a packet out of him, far more than she would have done for selling her stupid story—and he still wasn't sure that she didn't mean to go through with it. He shook his head. He didn't know what to think any more.

'It was the plan,' he agreed.

'But you'd changed your mind?'

'No!' It was a short, sharp response. He had to convince himself as well as Nicole that he'd done no such thing.

'So I don't see why you're making such a big issue out of what you *thought* I was going to do.'

'You deceived me.'

'I did not,' she retorted. 'What I was thinking and what I did are two separate things. And if you don't believe me then that's your hard luck.'

He wanted to believe her, so much he wanted to, but some little gremlin in the back of his mind told him that he'd be foolish to give in. In any case, if she didn't love him what was the point in even thinking about anything permanent?

'If you have nothing more to say I'll go and see if Tilda needs me.' Her chin was high, her lovely blue eyes bright. He would have liked to think they were bright with unshed tears—but why should she cry over him?

Ross waved a hand. 'You can go.' He should, of course, have told Nicole that he was sorry for doubting her integrity, but he didn't. He sat there quietly, unhappily, long after she'd gone.

Then all of a sudden Nicole came running back into his study, her face deeply distressed. 'Ross,' she said breathlessly, 'it's Tilda. She— I think she's…'

He leapt to his feet and bounded up the stairs, and when he saw his aunt he barked at Nicole to call the doctor.

Nicole stayed on at Court House until the funeral, helping Ross with the arrangements and consoling Aaron as best she could. But afterwards, once friends and relatives had gone and they were alone, she did what she knew she must do. 'My job here is finished,' she said to Ross, keeping a tight control on her emotions, knowing that she had to be strong. 'I'm going back to the flat.'

'So soon?' Ross looked at her as though she'd dealt him a body blow, although she knew he didn't really care. And his next words proved it. 'How about Aaron? You can't leave him now. He's brokenhearted about Tilda. If you go as well he'll—'

'I've done the job you paid me for,' she told him bluntly. 'You should have thought of Aaron's feelings before you employed me.' Lord, it hurt her to say this, because she loved that little boy as if he were her own. But the break had to come sooner or later, so best to do it now.

Since he'd accused her of deceiving him they'd each kept their distance, doing what had to be done, speaking only when necessary. And although she didn't want to go, although she'd like to stay and try and sort things out between them, she saw no point. Ross was determined to believe the worst of her.

'But who's going to look after him?' he asked.

She lifted her chin, hardening her heart. 'I suggest you employ a nanny. A proper nanny. He'll soon get used to her. Meantime you'll have to do it yourself. I've already packed. I'll be on my way.'

How she walked out of Court House without begging

and pleading with him to believe she'd meant him no harm, Nicole didn't know. But she had her pride. She might be hurting inside but her head was high as she left.

Ross came to the car with her. He carried her bags and stowed them in the boot and then he stood beside her as she opened her door. 'I'll be in touch with my solicitor,' he announced coolly. 'You'll get your divorce as soon as is legally possible. Thank you for all that you've done.'

She looked up at him, meeting the dark depths of his wonderfully thick-lashed eyes, feeling her nerve ends shudder, feeling the familiar weakness that always took over whenever he was close.

This was his last chance to beg her to stay. He'd said a few days ago that he couldn't fight his feelings. She'd felt a wicked elation. Had they been so shallow that they'd dried up and gone in the face of what he'd discovered? If he truly felt anything for her surely he would have believed her. It looked as though it was lust all along that had motivated him.

'The sooner the better as far as I'm concerned,' she retorted, and slid into the car, slamming the door and turning the key in the ignition. She didn't wind down the window, she didn't wave, she simply drove away.

Through her rearview mirror she saw him standing there, watching her, a lone figure against the backdrop of Court House, and she knew that this picture of him would be with her for the rest of her life.

Nicole hadn't been able to wait to get away from him. This thought tormented Ross for days. He didn't go to the office. He stayed at home with Aaron, who moped and grumbled and was as out of sorts with the world as his grandfather.

He understood about Tilda, accepted that she'd gone to heaven to join his mummy, but he kept asking when Nicole was coming back, and Ross's answer was always a terse, 'She's not.'

'But why has she gone?'

He could never answer that one, so usually said instead, 'She didn't tell me.'

'Doesn't she love me any more? Did I do something wrong? Is it my fault?' Tears welled again in Aaron's eyes.

Ross pulled his grandson to him. 'It's me who did something wrong. She still loves you dearly. I expect she'll write to you.'

'But I want to see her. Now! What did you do, Grandpa, that made her go away?'

'I didn't tell her I loved her,' he answered sadly. And now he had lost her.

In the weeks that followed, despite trying to dismiss Nicole from his mind, Ross found himself thinking about her constantly. With the resilience of the very young Aaron was back to his normal self, but Ross felt dreadful.

He couldn't eat, he couldn't sleep, and he was no good at the office. He couldn't make any decisions, he couldn't tackle any problems, he was good for nothing. The maxim that throwing yourself into your work made you forget your troubles simply didn't work.

'For pity's sake, man,' said Mark on more than one occasion, 'pull yourself together. She's not the only fish in the sea.'

But she was the only one Ross wanted.

He gradually came to the conclusion that denying himself Nicole was the wrong thing to do. What point was there in spending the rest of his life alone and embittered?

Even if fate— No, he would not think that way any more. It was a destructive emotion. He must be positive.

But what if Nicole didn't want him? He hadn't treated her well, in fact he'd behaved abominably towards her. And had he really believed that she'd write a story about him?

No. He'd wanted to; that was the problem. He'd grasped at the excuse because he was afraid of being too happy, too involved.

She'd phoned Aaron a couple of times while he'd been at the office, so he hadn't heard the wonderful husky tones of her voice. She'd chosen her moments well, guessing he'd be out, making it obvious that she was trying to avoid him.

And then, a few days before Christmas, came a letter, blunt and to the point.

Dear Ross,
I've not heard from your solicitor yet. I wish to know how soon I'm getting my divorce. It's very important to me. Let me know.
Nicole.

She'd found someone else! She'd met another man and wanted to marry him! But she couldn't, she mustn't. He wanted her, she was his, he intended to keep her.

The truth of the matter was that he'd not even contacted his solicitor. He'd been deliberately dragging his heels. He asked Mark as soon as he got to the office whether Marie had said anything about Nicole having another boyfriend.

'Not a word,' his partner answered. 'All Marie says is that she's unhappy. That she's hardly eating and—'

'Why the hell didn't you tell me this before?' Ross cut in urgently.

'Because you never asked. Besides, I thought...'

His words weren't heard because Ross had snatched up his jacket and rushed from the room.

Nicole was unhappy! It could mean only one thing. That their parting was upsetting her as much as it was him. He had to rectify it. He had to see her. He had to put things right.

Ross had no idea what he was going to say as he pulled

up outside the house. The three girls lived in the top-floor flat and no one could get in unless they buzzed up first. But as he approached a young woman came out of the main door and he managed to slip inside before the door closed. She looked at him curiously but made no attempt to stop him.

Outside Nicole's door he straightened his tie and tidied his hair with his fingers; he took a deep breath, and knocked. No one answered. Damn! Don't say she was out. He knocked again. A faint voice called, 'Who is it?'

'It's Ross.' It was almost like being a teenager again on his first date, not quite knowing how to handle himself.

It felt like hours before he heard any movement. It was probably only a minute, but it was the longest minute of his life. Finally the door opened a fraction and she peered round the edge of it. 'What do you want?'

'I got your letter. We need to talk.' And, when she showed no sign of letting him in, 'Please, Nicole, it's important.' He put his hand on the door and pushed, expecting resistance, grateful when she stood back and allowed him to enter.

He'd never been inside the girls' flat before, but this was no time for looking around. He was aware of a Christmas tree near the window, and strings of cards on the walls, but it was Nicole who concerned him. She looked truly awful, her face pale and drawn, and she was dressed in an old pair of leggings and a baggy sweater that had seen better days. 'Are you all right?' he enquired.

'I'm fine,' she assured him firmly.

'You don't look it.'

'If you'd let me know you were coming I'd have dressed for the occasion,' she told him scathingly. 'What do you want to say that couldn't be put in a letter?'

'That I'm sorry.' More than sorry, he was full of remorse and self-recrimination. He hated himself. Looking back, it had been the height of callousness insisting she marry him and sign a contract saying they were both free to walk out at the end of Tilda's life.

He'd upheld none of it. He'd said he wouldn't touch her, and what had he done? Made love. Not once but many times. His hormones surged at the thought of it. He'd hated lying in an empty bed these last weeks, had missed the soft, pleasurable warmth of her, the exciting earthy sexiness of her, the—

'Sorry for what?' Her voice cut into his thoughts, her beautiful voice that had enchanted him from the very beginning. 'As far as I'm concerned our contract was carried out and completed. You have nothing to be sorry for.'

'Shall we sit down?' he said.

'Yes, of course.' She seemed surprised at her own inhospitality.

They chose chairs well away from each other. Or at least Nicole chose to sit away from him. He would have preferred the settee, together. He wanted to inhale her special fragrance, to hold her hands, to assure her that he would never treat her badly again.

But first of all, of course, he needed to find out what her feelings were for him. There was no point in opening his heart only to have it thrown back in his face.

'Aaron's missing you, Nicole.'

At last a faint smile. 'Is he? I thought he'd have forgotten me by now.'

'I don't think he'll ever forget you.' And nor will I.

'Did you find him a nanny?'

'Yes.'

'Is she—good with him?'

'He seems to like her. But not as much as he liked you. Won't you come and see him some time?' He was watching her face closely and thought he saw wistfulness. 'He asks where you are frequently. He seems to think it's his fault that you left.' It was wrong bringing the boy in to tug at her heartstrings, but drastic needs meant drastic measures.

Nicole looked pained at his suggestion. 'What did you tell him? Poor thing. I hope you put him right?'

Ross grimaced and nodded briefly. 'I said it was my fault for not—for not treating you as well as I should have done.'

'Your treatment of me wasn't why I left. The job was over; it's as simple as that.'

But he noticed that she didn't look him in the eye as she spoke. 'Oh, Nicole, I wish I could believe that. You rushed off so quickly that I felt sure there were other reasons. I thought you'd grown to hate me because—'

'No!'

The single emphatic word filled him with joy.

'I don't hate you, Ross. I've never hated you.'

'Can we be friends again?'

She frowned. 'What sort of friends?'

He was putting this badly, he knew, but for the first time in his life he was at a loss as to how to handle the situation. 'Whatever sort you'd like.'

'Platonic?'

His heart took a nosedive. 'If that's all you're offering.'

'You want more?'

He wondered if he looked as uncomfortable as he felt. 'Er, yes. You can't deny that we were good in bed together, Nicole. More than good—fantastic. *You* were fantastic. I'll admit it. I can't get you out of my mind.'

'And that's all you want me for—a good time in bed?' Her eyes had suddenly turned glacial.

Oh, God, he'd said the wrong thing. 'No, of course not. Please, Nicole, don't think that.'

'What am I supposed to think?'

'I'm making a bad job of this, I know,' he told her with a grimace, 'but the truth of the matter is I don't want our marriage to end.'

She looked at him for several long seconds before asking quietly, 'Why?'

It was the moment for truth. He'd not managed this very well at all. He'd found out nothing about her own feelings. What if she laughed in his face? What if she told him to get lost, that she never wanted to see him again? How could he handle that once he'd made his admission?

But she was still waiting for his answer, and he knew he had to speak now because he'd never get another opportunity. He took a deep breath and said the words he'd vowed never to say again. 'Because I love you, Nicole.'

He was afraid to look at her, terrified of rejection. This woman meant as much to him as Alison had done, maybe even more. She had filled his life with so much joy, so much pleasure, that these last few weeks it had been as though a light had gone out.

When she said nothing he finally looked at her—and to his amazement saw tears coursing down her cheeks. He was on his feet immediately and across the room. 'Nicole, Nicole. What's the matter?' He pulled out a handkerchief and, perching on the arm of the chair, he dabbed at her tears.

'Tell me what's wrong,' he urged. 'I didn't mean to upset you.'

She looked at him through her tear-misted eyes, and her smile was like that of an angel. 'They're tears of joy.'

He looked at her like some half-crazed idiot. 'I don't understand.'

'Because—' she stroked a hand down his cheek and it felt as though she was making love '—it means my baby's going to have a father after all.'

'What? Your baby? My baby? Our baby? You're going to have a baby?' It was too much to take in. He stood up and began to pace the room, the tiny room with its unstimulating view of dirty chimneypots. And then he stopped in front of her and looked down. 'You're having my baby?'

She smiled serenely now. 'That's what I said.'

'But how—when—? We've always been careful.'

'Except for that first time.'

'Do you mind?' He was scared now that she might hold it against him.

'Ross, would I be behaving like this if I minded?'

'Did you know before you walked out on me?'

'No.'

'Would you have told me?'

'Maybe one day.'

'Damn! Thank God I came. Oh, Nicole, this is wonderful news. This is the best Christmas present I could ever have.' And then he stopped. 'It is, isn't it?' He was still beset with worries. She'd turned his world upside down. He didn't know what to think any more.

'Come here,' she said in her husky, sexy voice. 'Come and hold me, kiss me, let me tell you how much I love you.'

It stopped him in his tracks. 'You do?'

'Of course, you idiot,' she retorted with a laugh as she rose from her chair. 'You don't think I'd have told you about the baby if I didn't.'

He groaned as she reminded him about the unborn child, his child, and clapped a hand to his brow. 'To think I almost didn't come.' He wouldn't have done if Mark hadn't told him that she was unhappy. The consequences didn't bear thinking about. But there was still something else that needed to be said.

'Nicole,' he said quietly, almost too quietly he could see her straining to hear his words. 'I made a pledge to myself when Alison died that I'd never fall in love again.'

'So—what are you trying to say?' she asked, her smile

fading. 'That loving me is a mistake? That you don't want to remain married to me after all?'

'No!' He shook his head. 'Not that, Nicole. Never! I've fallen in love with you despite my reservations. But there's another problem I've not told you about. I have this great fear. Everyone I've ever loved in my life has died young. Grandparents, parents, wife, daughter. And I'm afraid to put you in that position. If I lost you as well then life wouldn't be—'

'Ross.' Nicole took his face between her palms and forced him to look at her. 'It won't be like that,' she said urgently.

'But we don't know.' There was a depth of anguish in his voice that he couldn't hide.

'I know I love you, Ross Dufrais. And *I'm* not afraid. There are no guarantees in this life—for anyone. *You* could get knocked down by a bus and *I'd* be left alone. They're the risks we have to take. And if we love each other then I think they're worthwhile.'

He drew in a deep, unsteady breath. 'You're an amazing woman.'

'It's why you've fallen in love with me,' she said with an impish grin. 'I'm irresistible.'

'You're that all right,' he agreed. And very gently, as though she were a precious piece of porcelain, he took her into his arms and kissed her.

He didn't believe in all that romantic rubbish about time standing still and bells in heaven ringing—but something was certainly happening to him. He felt quite unsteady on his feet, and with trembling hands he propelled Nicole back to the chair where he sat her on his lap.

'Tell me I'm not dreaming.'

She touched a kiss to her fingers and placed it on his lips. 'You're not dreaming. I think maybe I am. I never imagined for one moment that you were in love with me.'

'I think I was a little in love with you the day we first met. It was your voice that did it. It's so sexy, so—oh, let's not bother with words.' And he kissed her again and again and again.

It was a long time later before he said, 'I think we're going to make one little boy very very happy.'

'Not as happy as you've made me, Ross. You'd better stop the divorce.'

He pulled a wry face. 'As a matter of fact I never did anything about it. I think deep down I was hoping we'd get back together, despite my reservations.'

'You've no more fears that love is a dangerous emotion?'

'Oh, it's dangerous all right,' he told her. 'Deadly dangerous. You've no idea what you do to me.'

'And you to me,' she whispered, smiling. 'But I think we ought to check up on it. Make sure that everything still works properly.'

'I thought you'd never ask, Mrs Dufrais. Lead the way.'

'Oh, no, not the bedroom,' she said. 'Here, now. Take me, Ross. Make me yours again.'

And he did. Again and again and again.

They were now husband and wife in the truest sense of the words, and finally Ross put his fears to rest that she was going to be taken away from him. He was a truly happy man.

HARLEQUIN®
INTRIGUE
WE'LL LEAVE YOU BREATHLESS!

If you've been looking for thrilling tales of contemporary passion and sensuous love stories with taut, edge-of-the-seat suspense—then you'll love Harlequin Intrigue!

Every month, you'll meet four new heroes who are guaranteed to make your spine tingle and your pulse pound. With them you'll enter into the exciting world of Harlequin Intrigue— where your life is on the line and so is your heart!

THAT'S INTRIGUE—
ROMANTIC SUSPENSE
AT ITS BEST!

HARLEQUIN®
Makes any time special ®

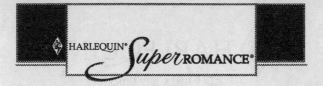

HARLEQUIN®
Makes any time special®

HARLEQUIN®
AMERICAN *Romance* — Upbeat, All-American Romances

HARLEQUIN®
Duets™ — Romantic Comedy

Harlequin® Historical — Historical, Romantic Adventure

HARLEQUIN®
INTRIGUE — Romantic Suspense

Harlequin Romance® — Capturing the World You Dream Of

HARLEQUIN®
Presents~ — Seduction and passion guaranteed

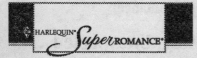
HARLEQUIN® *Super*ROMANCE® — Emotional, Exciting, Unexpected

HARLEQUIN®
Temptation — Sassy, Sexy, Seductive!